TOUCH OF POWER

JULIE ALSPAUGH

DEDICATION

This book is dedicated to my parents
who encouraged me to pursue God first as I
learned to use the gifts He had given.

CHAPTER 1

Valarie looked up through her tears and took her dad's hand. He led her out to his tool area in the garage. Stooping, he lifted his dark haired three-year-old and set her on the smooth wood of the workbench. He smiled at her. Thanks to her mother, she was dressed in a bright yellow play dress with matching sunflower leggings. Her short dark hair was braided in two short braids that barely reached her shoulders. There was no trace of her smile which was usually as bright as the sunflowers she wore. Taking the doll from her arms, he gently turned it over to inspect the back of it.

"Your baby didn't die, Valarie," he told her gently. "Your baby is a toy. She is fun to play with, but she isn't alive."

"She doesn't laugh anymore," Valarie insisted, rubbing her eyes. "Mommy said you can fix her."

Zach Calgen looked into his daughter's dark, serious eyes. "This baby has a special box with power in it. That is what made her laugh and cry. She just ran out of power."

"Can you put more in?" Valarie leaned forward with interest to watch the operation.

"Sure I can." Zach smiled at her confidently. Opening the velcro holding the cloth over the battery pack inside the doll, Zach scanned the peg board and selected a screw driver. "This screw is what holds the batteries in."

"What are batteries?" Valarie asked. The closer she looked, the harder it was for Zach to see the screw.

"A battery is a little container that holds power or electricity in it. Like when you turn on the light switch, that lets the power go to the light bulb in the ceiling. Baby dolls can't be stuck to the wall, so they put a little bit of electricity into…" he dropped the tiny screw into a clear plastic cup on the workbench where he could find it later. Removing the cover, he pulled out one of the batteries. "They put the electricity into this." Zach held the ends of the battery with his thumb and index finger, holding it up for her to see. "The battery holds electricity, and each time your baby laughs she uses a little of that power. When it is used up, she can't laugh anymore."

"How do you make electricity, Daddy?" Valarie had already forgotten the heartbreak that had swallowed her world only moments before. She swung her legs and picked up her doll to examine the inside of the battery case.

"Um… That's a good question, Honey." Zach was checking the drawers of his tool cabinet. "People make electricity by capturing different kinds of energy." Pulling a single battery from the last drawer, he shuffled the contents around to see if there was another. There was not. Seeing Valarie's expectant look, he went on explaining as he looked through the items on the shelf. "Some people use energy from the sun, or the wind, or things that God made. They can get that power and use it to make other things run."

"Like babies?" Valarie was sticking her little fingers in the battery slots.

"Yeah, dolls and lights and all kinds of things," he answered distractedly, still searching. He had only one battery and the doll took two.

"I can make electricity too," Valarie told him proudly.

Zach paused his rummaging through the bins beneath the workbench to look up at the three-year-old beaming down at him. "You can? Well that is handy. You definitely seem to have an endless supply of energy." Moving to the upper shelf, he asked, "How do you make it?"

"With my tummy." She said it matter-of-factly, and Zach could not help smiling.

"Val, Daddy only has one battery, but your baby needs two. Would it be terrible to wait to replace them until I go to the store tonight?"

"She couldn't laugh all day?"

"Just until tonight, I'll go right after dinner. I need to finish cleaning up the yard while there is still light to see."

She turned her doll over and looked at its face. "I don't think I could bear it."

Zach turned away to hide his silent laughter. "Well, why don't you put a little of that energy you make into that dead battery and fill it back up." Spotting a box he had missed, he dug around in it half-heartedly, knowing there were no batteries inside.

Looking thoughtful, Valarie stuck the end of the AA battery into her mouth.

"Honey, she's eating it!" Brook cried from the doorway of the garage.

Zach spun and snatched the dead battery from Valarie's mouth. "No, no, no. You can't put them in your mouth. Batteries have chemicals in them that will kill you." Zach picked up the second dead battery just in case. He looked at Brook. "Honey, is it actually possible for a kid to swallow an AA battery?"

"That's not the point, Zach," Brook pointed out. "We don't want Valarie eating any size battery." She turned her attention to the little girl who was taking it all in with wide eyes. "Valerie, if you swallowed a battery, we would have to rush you to the hospital, and they might have to cut you open to get it out. Batteries inside you are very, very bad." She glanced at her husband and added, "Especially little batteries."

Valarie looked from one parent to the other. "Then how do I fill it?"

Brook looked at Zach questioningly.

"She makes electricity with her tummy," Zach explained with a suppressed grin. "It is good to talk about things with your three-year-old because sometimes they have super powers you didn't expect."

Her eyebrows went up in surprise, and she looked amused. "How do you know you can make electricity, Valarie?"

Valarie shrugged.

"The annoying cow toy!" Zach exclaimed. "We put it up in the closet, remember? It has AA batteries in it." He set the dead batteries on the workbench by Valarie. "Don't put them in your mouth. I'll be right back."

"How is Baby?" Brook asked coming to put her hand on the doll laying across her daughter's lap.

"She is not dead but she needs power to laugh," Valarie informed her mom, reaching for the batteries Zach had left.

"Don't put them in your mouth," Brook instructed, handing them to her.

"I won't." She stretched her little hand trying to touch both ends of the battery at once.

"Honey, I can't find that cow," Zach called from inside. "Any ideas?"

"Look on the left side, in that grey shoebox," Brook called. "I had better go help him. Remember not to put the batteries into your mouth. I'll just be a minute."

"Okay, Mommy," Valarie was focused on the battery she held between her thumb and little finger.

A few minutes later, Zach returned followed by Brook. "Here we are!" he announced, putting the hot pink plastic cow on the workbench.

"I really need to clean out that closet." Brook put her hands on her hips and looked around the garage. "And this place could use it too."

"We have to finish the yard first," Zach reminded her, pulling the batteries from the cow. "Once we get this baby laughing again."

"I put electric power in these." Valarie held out the old batteries in her cupped palm.

"Um…" Zach glanced at his wife for help.

Brook shrugged. "It doesn't hurt to give them a try." She smiled. Grandma would enjoy this story.

"Right, it doesn't hurt to try them, does it?" He repeated, taking the batteries from Valarie. Clicking one into place, he hesitated, looking at the remaining battery in his hand.

"Are you nervous?" Brook was studying him with an amused expression.

"What if she can make power?" Zach asked seriously. "Wouldn't that be wild?"

"Want me to help you put it in?" Valarie asked, putting her little hand onto her dad's.

"Sure, let me line it up and you can click it in. Just remember these batteries were already used up."

She smiled up at him, "But I filled them up again."

"Right. Go ahead and push that one in."

She pushed, and Zach helped guide it into place.

"Now we turn her over,"

"No, Daddy, you have to close her back first." Valarie reached for the screwdriver.

"Right, confidence is key." He glanced back at Brook who was putting bins back up onto the shelves where they belonged.

"Okay, there you are," Zach closed up the velcro back and handed Baby to Valarie. "Give her a squeeze."

The recorded laugh echoed in the quiet garage. Brook met her husband's wide eyes. He was as shocked as she was.

"Thank you, Daddy!" Valarie hugged him, and he dumbly lowered her to the floor. She skipped away leaving her open-mouthed parents to try to piece together what they had just witnessed.

CHAPTER 2

"Mom! Tell Valarie to stop changing the channel. It is my turn to pick the show."

"Valarie, give the remote to your brother," Brook called from the kitchen.

Seven-year-old Valarie shot Trent a triumphant grin.

"Okay, Mom." She called, her eyes on the remote in his hand.

"I'll tell," Trent threatened softly.

Valarie gave him a withering look, "You had better not. You promised."

"You keep changing the show and I'll tell anyway." Trent was mad. He had already missed the lion catching the gazelle and felt the injustice deeply.

"Alright, watch your dumb animals eating each other." Valarie got up. Feeling restless, she went to the kitchen to see if her mom would offer her any entertainment.

Brook glanced over from her task and saw Valarie's bored expression. "Want to help me peel eggs for tomorrow's egg salad?"

"Not really." She fiddled with her mom's phone that lay on the counter, turning it slowly around on the counter with her finger. The screen lit up, and Valarie glanced at it.

"He's five, Valarie. Give him a chance to grow up too. Having the remote was a big deal for you too." Brook laughed, "Your Dad and I put up with a lot of silly cartoons when you turned five and got to pick the show."

Valarie couldn't help smiling a little, but it didn't stick. "Is there anything I can do?"

"You have about an hour before bed. Why don't you go tinker with those electronics in the garage? That always seems to charge you up."

"Mom," Valarie groaned at the bad pun. "We already have three working VHS players, and they don't even make VHS movies anymore. I want something interesting to do."

"Well, there's always the chore list," Brook offered.

Valarie groaned again. "That's not what I mean."

Brook leaned over and looked at the hand written list on the refrigerator door. "Ah, now I see why you two have been so good. The next job is a doozy, isn't it?"

Valarie sighed heavily, "There's nothing fun to do."

Brook noticed her daughter aimlessly rotating the phone on the counter with one finger.

"I need to charge that or we will be in a pickle tomorrow when we take Trent to his ball game. It is at that new field." Brook rinsed the egg she had finished peeling and got another from the carton. "You sure you don't want to help peel?"

Valarie was staring thoughtfully at the phone.

"You are awfully quiet. Is something on your mind?" Brook had finished another egg. "I could tell you stories about when you were little?"

"No, thank you, I'll find something else to do." She pushed herself away from the counter and wandered back into the living room where she flopped onto the couch. More lions were chasing more deer. She knew better than to mess with the TV. Trent was in a mood, and her secret would be out. She had learned to send an electrical signal to change the channel, but her parents were still a little unnerved when she made electricity. Even though Valarie had been doing it for four years now. They asked her not to tell other kids, no one except her best friend Jessie who already knew. Sometimes she heard them worrying about her at night when they thought she was asleep. They had called it an incredible power and were afraid people would try to exploit her for it. Her mom's phone had said exploit meant to abuse or manipulate someone for personal gain.

"Valarie?"

"Yes, Ma'am?"

"Could you come in here for a minute?"

"Sure," Valarie pulled herself up from the couch.

When she entered the kitchen, Brook was holding her phone. "Did you charge this?"

Valarie shrugged.

"The battery was at 5% and now it is at 100%."

The door opened, and Zach came in with a gust of crisp fall air. "Wow, sorry I'm late. It is windy out there! You should have seen that store. I stopped by for the mayonnaise you asked for, and everybody and their dog was out tonight." He grinned at Valarie, "There really was a dog in a cart." He set down the paper bag on the table. "I was hoping there had not been a dog in the cart I picked. I can understand service dogs, but these mangy little things that growl at everyone who passes are a disgrace to the dog kind."

Brook and Valarie grinned at each other. Zach did not appreciate dogs. The only ones he liked were stuffed animal type mounded on his son's bed. Trent, on the other hand, loved dogs more than anything. With the exception of watching hunting lions.

"What's in the bag?" Brook asked with a knowing smile.

Valarie peered into the bag and squealed with delight. "Trent, stop watching animals die. Dad got ice cream!"

"Valarie, Micah is sleeping. If he wakes up now..."

The TV powered off, and Trent came running. "Can we have ice cream now? Please, Dad? Just a little bit?"

"The baby is sleeping," Brook reminded them.

They lowered their voices, but their excitement rose as Zach pulled the carton of ice cream from the paper bag.

"You can give him a little bit. I want loads of it!" Valarie laughed hugging her dad.

The mood of the room had changed instantly. Brook smiled at her family. Her eyes drifted to the phone once more. Every week she discovered something more Valarie could do with her hidden power. What bothered her was that Valarie never wanted to talk about it.

———

"I saw on the news that you got your man," Zach said casually. He was holding up the board his Dad was screwing into place.

Reese Calgen had come to help his son repair the kids' fort that had been damaged by a dead tree limb, not to discuss the news. He only grunted in response.

"They said you were a hero," Zach tried again. Conversations with his dad were usually awkward and stiff. Looking at Reese, Zach felt a twinge of sadness. How often he had longed for his father to stop and notice him. As the youngest of four, Zach had not seen his father much during his formative years. Reese's fame and reputation as a detective grew faster than his son and soon left the latter behind. Never leaving a mystery unsolved meant late nights, early mornings, and stakeouts that lasted for days. The job always came first. Zach had learned to cope without him, but the hurt still lingered beneath the surface pleasantries. "Is it true, though, that they haven't located the body?"

Reese did not respond. His drill drowned out their conversation for a minute.

"I bet you were relieved to have caught up with him."

"Zach," Reese stopped working to look at his grown son.

Zach glanced at his dad expectantly.

"Let's leave the work at work. Okay?"

"Okay." Zach turned away to hide his disappointment. Brook told him to keep trying, but he didn't see any hope of ever connecting with his dad.

CHAPTER 3

"Whatcha doin'?" Valarie asked softly at Trent's door.

He looked up from his comic book with a guilty look. "Nothing."

Grinning she came into his room. "Reading, eh? That's very scholarly." Valarie strolled around his room examining his belongings as if it were a museum. "I guess you won't be interested in what I did."

"You turned off the TV with your mind?" Trent asked in a bored tone. "You are supposed to be in bed."

"Nope, that's not new," Valarie responded, ignoring his last statement.

"What then?" Trent lowered his comic book warily.

"This." Grinning excitedly, Valarie produced a lightbulb from her bulging pajama pocket. Holding the lightbulb by the metallic base she held it up. "Behold!"

"Oh wow, you can hold a…" Trent's eyes widened as the lightbulb lit up in her hand. "Oh wow," he repeated softly.

———

"Hello, hello! Look who's here!"

"Grandpa Calgen!" Trent plowed into his legs, hugging him tightly.

Reese Calgen's dark face creased into an easy smile. He put his hand on the door frame to steady himself. "Whoa there, you could knock an old man right off his feet. Hi there, Valarie!"

Valarie came from the living room with a bright smile. "Grandpa Calgen, we thought you would never get here!" She hugged him gently and then stepped back.

"Let go of him Trent. Let him at least come into the house." Zach stood on the porch behind his dad. His imitation leather briefcase hung from his shoulder. "Hi Dad!"

"Still using that old bag, huh?" Reese thumped his son on the back.

Smiling, Zach adjusted the shoulder strap. "It fits the bill."

"It's starting to show some wear. I'll see if I can get the commissioner to give me another one," Reese joked. Trent released him, and they all piled into the kitchen. The savory smell of the roast filled the house.

"A man alone can't make things smell as good as a woman can," Reese told his son. He had lost his wife to cancer a year ago and missed her more than he let on.

The table was set and ready for dinner. Brook emerged from the bedroom and greeted her father-in-law. "I knew if I stepped out to change Micah's diaper you would come. It is good to have you!"

Reese took the baby's chubby hand in his big, rough one, "And how is the little man?" He was rewarded by a drooling grin from Micah.

"Are you on a detective case, Grandpa?" Trent asked, bouncing on one foot." Did you catch the bad guys?"

"Dad has never missed his man," Zach interjected proudly. Inside he cringed. He wanted his kids to know their grandpa and love him. He hoped his own hurt would not taint their relationship.

"No, Trent," Reese laughed. "I haven't taken any new cases this week. Seems that the criminals these days aren't as smart as they used to be. They have taken the mystery out of crime."

"I suppose that is good for the police," Zach observed.

Reese chuckled, "I suppose so, but it makes a detective need to take his belt in a few notches."

"Come, sit, everything is ready." Brook did not have to tell them twice. Zach put Micah into his highchair, and the others found their places.

"Why does grandpa have to tighten his belt?" Trent asked in a whisper.

"Because there are no mysteries, so no one is paying him to figure them out," Valarie whispered back.

"What does that have to do with his belt?"

"When you don't get paid, you don't eat," Reese answered from across the table. He grinned at their surprised looks. "It is just an expression. I've got plenty to eat. My problem is I'm having to loosen my belt now that I've been coming here once a week." He turned his attention to Brook. "You are a fine cook, Brook."

"Thank you, Reese." She put a spoon into the potatoes and surveyed the table one last time before taking her seat.

"It looks amazing, Honey." Zach held out his hand to her. "Let's thank the Lord for all this wonderful food."

They bowed their heads as Zach prayed. Micah banged his spoon on his tray and looked around to see everyone's reaction. He giggled when Trent peeked at him with one eye.

"Micah doesn't know about being quiet when we pray," Trent explained once the prayer was over.

Putting his napkin into his lap, Reese glanced over at Micah. "Oh, he will catch on eventually."

"What is new for you these days, Dad?" Zach asked, spooning a dollop of potatoes onto Micah's tray.

"Oh, not much. Still working on keeping that scraggly garden alive. I don't know how your mom did it, Zach. She could get that plot to produce anything."

"If you need any produce, our tomatoes are going overboard this year," Brook offered, looking up from the bread she was buttering.

"We have another cantaloupe too!" Trent added excitedly.

"Maybe I should come take some gardening lessons from your mom."

Brook shook her head as she passed the rolls to Valarie. "You would have to get the tips from your son, Reese. He is the gardener of the family. I only pick the produce."

"Well, he didn't get that from me." Reese looked over at Zach as if seeing him for the first time.

"Mom taught me." There was something in the way Zach said it that took the wind out of the conversation. They fell silent, enjoying the food.

"What about you? Anything new in your neck of the woods?" Reese asked hoping to get them talking again. "How are you kids doing at school?"

"I am a grade ahead in math!" Humility was not one of Trent's stronger qualities. "And I already know how to read. This year we get to study continents. My favorite is Africa. That is where the lions live. There are a lot of countries in Africa."

"You like lions, don't you?" Reese turned his attention to Valarie, "And what about you, young lady? How is school for you? Do you still like learning at home?"

She glanced up at him. "Yes, sir. I do like learning at home."

"Do you have many friends around here?" Reese asked when she offered no additional information.

"My best friend, Jessie, lives two houses down. We hang out a lot. Mostly she comes here, but sometimes I go to her house. Her mom works, so Jessie still comes here after school." Valarie had told him about Jessie many times before. Jessie and Valarie had been best friends since Jessie had moved there almost 4 years ago. Grandpa should have remembered. She saw her dad glance her way with an understanding look, but she did not meet his eyes.

"She has a bunch more friends too," Trent cut in. "They all laugh and giggle at the park together. My friends know how to play real games." As Trent babbled on about himself, Reese noticed Brook gave her daughter a reassuring smile. Valarie was quiet and did not join in the conversation willingly. She seemed to become more withdrawn the older she got. It concerned Reese who, after nine years, still had not gotten used to the homeschooling trend.

After dinner, Reese asked Zach to show him the garden. Knowing they wanted time to talk, Brook enlisted Valarie and Trent to help her clean up.

"I'm worried about Valarie, Zach," Reese said suddenly after he had half-heartedly observed the flourishing garden.

Zach frowned, "What do you mean, Dad?"

"She's quiet, too sober for a nine year old. It is like she has grown up too fast inside." Reese paused, searching his son's face. "Is there something I should know about?"

Zach stooped to pick up a vine tendril and took his time securing it to the wire lattice. "She's just growing up. Kids go through phases."

"Look me in the eye and tell me that," Reese challenged.

Looking at his dad, Zach answered defensively. "Look, Dad, Brook and I are doing the best we can."

"I'm not saying you are not doing a good job, Zach. I'm asking if Valarie is okay." Reese followed his son out through the garden gate. "This isn't a sudden thing, and you know it, Zach. She's lost her laughter."

Zach crossed his arms. "Dad, there's nothing I can tell you. Mom's death was hard on us all. Valarie has had a lot to carry, and we are doing our best to help her process. Growing up is tough."

Reese watched his son knowingly. "If I was questioning you for a case, Zach, I would say you are covering something up."

Zach dropped his arms to his sides and met the probing look of his dad, Detective Calgen. "This isn't one of your cases. This is my daughter. I'll tell you if there is anything you need to know."

CHAPTER 4

"Trent, go ask your grandpa if he wants to play checkers with you." Brook instructed. "I'll take Micah and get him ready for bed." She turned away from the window and took the last serving bowl from Valarie who was clearing the table.

Valarie went to the window and looked across the yard at her dad and grandpa. They stood facing one another. She could tell from a distance that there was tension between them.

"They are talking about me."

Brook turned at her daughter's soft statement. "Why do you think that, Valarie?"

"I saw the looks Grandpa gave me at dinner. He kept looking at me as if searching for clues."

"You have to remember that he has been a detective for years." Brook scooped the last of the potatoes into a plastic container as she spoke. "Searching for clues is so ingrained in him that I don't think he knows how to stop."

Trent joined the men outside, and their body language changed instantly.

Valarie handed the lid for the potatoes to her mom who snapped it into place.

"Why doesn't Dad like him?" Valarie looked out at them again. Her grandpa was smiling and joking with Trent as they walked toward the fort.

Closing the refrigerator, Brook looked toward the window. "Who?"

"Grandpa. Why don't Dad and Grandpa get along? Dad loved Grandma, but he always gets stiff when Grandpa is here."

Brook smiled, "I think you may have a little detective in you too. Come on, we can talk while I get Micah ready for bed."

Valarie followed her mom down the hall to the boy's room. Brook let Micah down to play in the floor, and Valarie sat beside her on Trent's bed.

"Valarie, your grandpa was very busy when your dad was growing up. There was a big crime ring, a lot of bad men working together to commit crimes. Grandpa worked very hard to track down those men and stop the crimes. That meant he was not home for your dad when he was your age. Your aunts and uncle got a lot more of Grandpa's time when they were growing up. I guess your dad felt he wasn't important enough to get grandpa's attention. That hurt him very deeply." Brook put her hand on Valarie's. "Your dad is so scared that he will be a bad dad for you. He loves you so much. He can see you are hurting, but he does not know how to help. Give him a chance to be the dad he wants to be."

Valarie looked down at her hands.

"Things we don't understand are hard to explain. Valarie, you don't have to carry it alone. Your inner power has helped me so much. It may seem like nothing to you, but I do notice." Brook pulled her phone from the back pocket of her jeans and pointed to the battery level. "You know my phone used to die all the time. But I can't remember the last time it has been under 50%. I haven't had to replace a single battery in Micah's or Trent's toys. You have been giving back in so many little ways. I wanted you to know that I notice. And I am so grateful you are a part of our family. Not because of what you can do, but because of who you are."

Brook reached over and drew Valarie into a tight hug. Valarie hugged her back.

"Valarie."

Valarie froze at her dad's firm tone. She knew instantly she was in trouble.

"Come in here," Zach instructed. "And turn on the light."

Valarie obeyed, stepping hesitantly into the living room and switching on the light manually. She could do it without the switch now, but did not think this was a good time to let him know. "Yes, Sir?"

Zach sat on the couch across from where she stood. "Is there anything you would like to tell me?" His expression was serious.

"I…" Valarie shifted uncomfortably. "I didn't know you were in here."

"I could tell," Zach observed. "You just changed your brother's channel as you passed, didn't you?" He did not miss the victorious smirk Trent gave his sister.

Valarie shifted again, not meeting his probing gaze.

"Where is the remote?"

She looked over at Trent.

"I have it. It is my night." Trent held it up.

"Turn off the TV."

Trent raised the remote, and the TV went off.

"I had it!" he protested.

Zach frowned slightly when he saw Valarie's surprised look. She had thought he was speaking to her. She had turned the TV off before Trent could push the power button.

"Come sit down." Zach patted the couch cushion beside him. "How long have you been able to do that?" Valarie chose to take the seat at the far end of the couch. She sat gingerly as if ready to fly from the room if needed. "I don't know."

"For years!" Trent cut in. "She does it all the time, and it is so annoying!"

"Trent, I'm talking to your sister," Zach pointed out.

"Well, I'm involved," Trent protested. "I've been suffering under her communism for years!"

"I think you mean tyranny," Valarie informed him with a hint of scorn.

Trent looked at his dad to see if the new word fit better.

"If you were suffering, why didn't you tell us?" Zach asked him.

"She said I couldn't," Trent answered quickly. "But it is so annoying! She's a freak."

"Trenten Reese Calgen that is a lie. If you ever say that about your sister again, the punishment chore list on the fridge will become your permanent chore list."

Trent's eyes got big, and he quickly closed his mouth. Zach did not need to say more. He kept his reproving eye on his son a little longer, causing the seven-year-old to squirm in his seat.

Zach rose and beckoned to Valarie, "Come with me, Valarie."

She followed him out to the garage.

He pulled out a camp chair, but Valarie hoisted herself up onto the workbench, swinging her legs slightly as she waited for the lecture.

It had been six years since the morning when his three-year-old daughter had sat where she was sitting now and had charged a battery that was not rechargeable. For six years, his daughter had been experimenting with her power, and he had known little to nothing about it. Fear had kept them from understanding the extent of what she could do. She had been shy and reserved about it, and Zach suspected she had overheard some late night conversations that were not meant for her ears. Not talking about it was only making things worse. As much as he hated to admit it, his dad was right. Valarie was pulling away from them. Zach was not going to let her slip away without a fight.

Putting his back against the workbench, Zach hopped up to sit beside her. "Valarie, do you remember the first time you told me about your power?"

She nodded.

"You said it came from your tummy."

Valarie glanced at him with a shy smile.

He was smiling too. "We haven't really talked about it much since then, but it is a big part of who you are." He looked into her deep brown eyes. "Valarie, will you help me to understand your gift?"

She looked away, her arms moved unconsciously as she hugged them to herself. "I don't know how."

"Do you mind if I ask questions?" Zach asked gently. "Will that help?"

"I don't want to be a freak, Dad." A tear slid down her cheek, and she quickly wiped it away.

He put his arm around her, and she scooted closer to him. "Valarie, you are not a freak. That is a lie. A cruel thing your brother said to get even with you for switching his shows. Words hurt so deeply. I can bet you anything that Trent is in there aching for you and wishing he hadn't said what he did."

"But it is true. No one else has electricity in their tummy." She did not look up, but he could hear the smile in her voice. She was changing the subject, gently turning the conversation away from what hurt.

"Look at me, Valarie." Zach waited until she obeyed. "You are not a freak. God created you perfectly to do amazing things that no one else can do. When I think of your gift, my mind is totally blown. You are so special, Valarie! I mean, I was born with double-jointed thumbs and thought that was special, but that's nothing compared to what God gave you."

She laughed a little and sniffed back her unshed tears.

Reaching across her, Zach pulled a thick blue paper towel

from the roll and handed it to her. "This is a man tissue."

She smiled at his lame joke. Taking the paper towel he offered, she blew her nose. "I don't know why God gave me this…"

"Gift," Zach finished for her. "Valarie, it is a gift. Until you believe that, you will never be able to use it fully for God's glory."

"I can't see how turning things off and on can bring God glory," Valarie responded, fiddling with the clean corner of the paper towel.

"That is the exciting part. I don't know why I have double-jointed thumbs either."

"Dad," Valarie laughed. "That's different."

"Yeah, it is." Zach was looking out over the cluttered garage. "Seriously, Val, I feel like I've done a terrible job at being your Dad. You were already this brilliant, gifted kid, and all of a sudden, you have a power I've never even imagined possible. Your gift amazed me," he glanced down at her and she met his gaze. His eyes moved back to the items on the shelf across the garage before he spoke again. "Honestly, Val, it scared me. I'm your dad. It is my job to protect you. Even though Grandpa didn't talk about it much, growing up with a detective for a dad made me aware of all kinds of bad guys out there." His arm around her tightened a little. "I want to keep you safe, Valarie. I'm not anything special, and I have no idea how to raise a daughter." He glanced down at her. "So how did I get the privilege of a beautiful girl like you with super powers?"

Her shy smile appeared once more.

"You see," Zach went on. "I've noticed lately that I have the same problem you had when you were three. My baby has stopped laughing." He paused to let it sink in. "It breaks my heart to see you carrying this alone."

She wiped her eyes with the paper towel.

"I guess I'm asking you if you will help me. And if you will let me help you."

Leaning her head against her dad, Valarie nodded.

CHAPTER 5

"Can you really change it?" Jessie asked crouching beside Valarie in the bushes.

"I could yesterday." Valarie answered. "But you still can't tell people. The promise still stands. I'm only telling you this because you are my very best friend and I trust you."

Jessie flipped her blond hair over her shoulder indignantly, "You don't have to say all that every time."

In looks, Jessie was completely opposite of Valarie. Valarie was dark and willowy, and Jessie was fair and sturdily built. They peered through the leaves to make sure they had not been overheard. Jessie's straight, blond hair stood out in sharp contrast to Valarie's thick, dark hair. Despite their differences, the girls were inseparable friends.

"I haven't told anyone yet, have I?" Jessie pointed out.

"You told your Dad that one time." Valarie reminded her.

"That was when I was six, Valarie. Three whole years ago. I am much better at keeping secrets now, so you can stop bringing that up. You know my dad asked me why we were turning the bedroom light on and off so much. I am not going to go tell people, but I couldn't lie to my parents." Jessie looked down. "I guess it didn't matter though. Dad lied to us."

Valarie gripped her friend's hand tightly. "He didn't leave because of you, Jessie."

"I know. Mom says that too. It still feels like I was the

reason. I tried to be everything he wanted, but it wasn't enough." Even thought it had happened years ago, Jessie's eyes still got moist when she talked about her parent's divorce. She glanced at Valarie and rubbed her eyes. "So I'm not going to tell about the traffic light. If," she added with a skeptical look, "you can actually change it."

"You don't believe me now, Jessie, but you will. I just don't want to worry my parents. Dad and I had a talk, you know."

"So why don't you tell him about this?" Jessie asked gesturing toward the street light.

"I will if it comes up." Valarie shrugged, fiddling with a dead twig to avoid meeting Jessie's gaze. "They still talk about me when they think I'm not around. And I hear them whispering about me in the night. They are worried I will get kidnapped or something. They even have this tracking bracelet I have to wear when I go out." Valarie covered the bracelet with her hand and looked embarrassed. "I don't want other people to know about it."

"Wow, those things are expensive." Pulling Valarie's hand off of the bracelet, Jessie examined it with admiration. "It is really small. Jacob's dog has one that is like this big." Jessie showed the size with both her hands. "Yours must have cost a ton. It doesn't look like a tracker at all." She looked at Valarie with a grin. "It's pretty sweet! Can I try it on?"

Valarie was undecided.

"Please, Valarie? I'll only wear it for a minute. It is so pretty."

Unclipping the bracelet, she handed it to Jessie who slipped her hand inside. "Wow, it is really comfortable too."

She was rewarded by a pleased smile from Valarie.

———

"Mrs. Calgen! Come quick. Someone took Valarie!" Jessie pounded desperately on the door. "Please help her!"

The door swung open, and Brook, with Micah on her hip, looked down at her daughter's best friend. Her face was pale and streaked with tears.

"He took her, Mrs. Calgen. He had a gun. I was so scared. I didn't know what to do."

"Who did he take?" Brook knew the answer by the tight knot of fear in her stomach.

"He took Valarie. He had a gun and made her get in the car."

"Oh, Lord, protect my baby." Brook handed the toddler to Jessie and ran for her phone.

Micah wailed in protest. Jessie, in a state of shock, kept her arms tightly around the squirming, screaming child.

Brook came back into the room with the phone to her ear.

"My daughter, Valarie Calgen. Yes, she was wearing, let me think, Jessie can you try to keep him quiet?" She was pacing and talking fast to the dispatch officer. Jessie clapped her hand over Micah's mouth, struggling to keep the toddler up with one arm. He squirmed expertly, determined to get away from her.

Brook looked over, and her eyes locked on the bracelet Jessie wore. "Jessie, where did you get that bracelet?" Brook demanded. She dropped the phone onto the table. Crossing the room, she took Micah from Jessie and gripped the girl's wrist. "Where did you get this?"

Jessie was crying hard now and doing her best to explain that she had only tried it on for a minute.

"What's the matter?" Trent asked from the doorway.

"Trent take your brother to the bedroom and play with him. Don't come out until I call you."

Trent's shoulders drooped. "Mom." He whined, drawing out the word.

"Now." There is a tone that Moms use which conveys better than words all the punishments that will come on a child who does not obey. This was the tone Brook used. Trent was seven now. He understood well the consequences of pushing his mom after she had used that tone. He took Micah and managed to wrestle the wailing two-and-a-half year old into the bedroom. The door shut, and the noise level dropped instantly.

Brook picked up the phone from the table. "Hello?" She listened for a moment. "No, no one is injured here. My daughter has been kidnapped…" Brook stopped pacing and pulled the sobbing Jessie into a hug. "Ma'am, no one here is injured." She paused, "That was my two-year-old. Yes, he's fine. Please stay focused. My daughter is in danger," Brook informed her with a forced calm. "Her friend said the man had a gun and made her get into his car." Brook paused. "Yes, she was wearing a yellow shirt with a sunshine, or a flower on the front." Brook looked down at Jessie.

"It was a smiling sunflower," Jessie told her.

"A yellow shirt with a smiling sunflower. Dark shorts, white shoes with yellow laces. Yes, dark hair. No, I don't remember how it was fixed." A movement caught her eye, and she saw Jessie moving her hand like a rainbow over her head and mouthing 'headband'. Jessie pulled on her own sleeve, and Brook remembered. "Valarie's hair was pulled back with a bright yellow headband… Yes… I'm her mom, Brook Calgen." Brook glanced at the bracelet Jessie had put on the table. "No, she is not wearing it… Alright… Yes, please ask them to hurry."

She hung up and sunk into a chair, keeping her arm around Jessie. Her fingers moved across the screen of her phone, and she put it to her ear once more. Her eyes were on the bracelet. "Zach?" It was all she could say. The tears came in shaky sobs. Her arm slipped from around Jessie, and she laid her head on the table, her hand covering her mouth as she wept.

"I'm sorry, Mrs. Calgen," Jessie whispered. "I didn't know what to do."

Brook could only shake her head.

Jessie took the phone from her. "Mr. Calgen?"

"Who is this?" Zach asked, his tone urgent.

"Jessie."

"Jessie?" he repeated thoughtfully, "Oh, right. Jessie, I'm almost to my car. What's going on?"

She could tell by his voice that he was running. "A man took Valarie. She doesn't have the bracelet on because she let me try it on right before the man came. I didn't know. I'm sorry."

"Have you called the police?"

A car door slammed in the background. Jessie heard the car start and the squeal of tires.

"Mrs. Calgen did. I think they are coming."

"Where did it happen?" Though Zach could feel the adrenaline pumping through his body, his mind was clear and focused.

"The park right by the intersection. Valarie was…" Jessie paused, remembering her promise.

"Jessie, I need you to tell me everything you know," Zach instructed. "There are times when a promise between friends must be broken to protect the friend from danger."

"Yes, Sir. That was part of the promise." Jessie took a deep breath. "She wanted to see if she could change the traffic lights."

Zach was silent. Charging phones, changing the TV channels without a remote, and turning on lights without using the light switch were things he and Valarie had talked about. Changing traffic lights was on a whole new level. "Is Brook okay?"

"She's crying a lot, Mr. Calgen. Please hurry."

"I'll be right there, and I'm bringing backup." Zach hung

up the phone and looked at the flashing police lights in his rearview mirror. "Yeah, you bet I'm speeding," Zach said in a low tone to the officer behind him. "Why don't you tag along and see why?"

CHAPTER 6

Reese Calgen heard the door handle turn and looked up from his computer. He smiled and rose to greet his son. "Zach, it has been a long time since you dropped by the office." His years as a detective kicked in, and Reese paused to study his son. "Everything okay?" Reese asked seriously.

Concern and perhaps a glint of fear were evident in Zach's features as he approached his father's thick mahogany desk. "Dad, we need to talk," Zach had made no effort to return his father's cheerful greeting.

Gesturing to one of the two chairs in front of his desk, Reese came around to sit in the other. "Sit down, Zach, tell me what is going on."

"Valarie has been kidnapped." For once Zach was grateful his dad had been around crime all his life. Instead of panicking, like any other grandparent would have done, Reese was calm and collected.

"You called the police?"

"Yes, Sir, as soon as we knew she was gone. They are looking for her now."

Reese went to his desk and pushed a button on his phone. "Nina, have you heard anything about a kidnapping come across the scanner in the last thirty minutes?" he glanced at his son for confirmation.

Zach nodded.

The phone chirped to life with a quick, "Yes, Sir, it came

through on channel 14 about twenty minutes ago. No updates yet."

"I want you to keep me informed if anything comes through that could be related to that case."

"Yes, Sir," Nina responded.

Reese poked another button to end the conversation. He picked up a notepad and pencil from the desk top. "It pays to have a secretary who listens to the police scanner like other ladies listen to the radio."

Nina had started working for Detective Reese Calgen the year after Zach and Brook were married, and she was slowly pulling the sixty year old man out of the dark ages. The updated, though still out of date, phone system was her doing. As well as the cell phone the detective now carried. Even with all the technological advances, Reese still preferred to take notes with a notepad and pencil. It was a battle she knew she would never win.

He took his seat beside Zach and flipped the notepad open. "Tell me what you know about it."

After they had covered the where, when, and how details, Reese set the pad of notes on his knee and looked intently at his son. "Now for the rest. What are you not telling me that may have a bearing on this case?"

Zach hesitated.

"Zach, the smallest details can mean life or death in a kidnapping situation. I'm asking you to trust me. Trust me as a detective if you cannot trust me as your father."

Taking a deep breath, Zach let it out forcefully. "Not long ago, you asked me about Valarie. I told you then that I would tell you if there was anything you needed to know." Zach looked down at a crease in his well ironed pants and cleared his throat nervously. "I should have told you sooner, Dad, but we weren't sure how to tell you."

"Don't worry about my feelings, Zach." Reese smiled a

little. "Pretend I'm just another detective, if that helps."

He was rewarded by a weak smile from Zach. It was a line he'd heard almost every day growing up. Reese Calgen, a man known for cracking the most complicated cases, would come home to his quiet normal house to be greeted by four rowdy kids and his wife. When they tried to pry the excitement of the day out of him, he would smile, shrug and say, "I'm just another private detective doing what detectives do."

"Zach, besides being my granddaughter, how else is Valarie special?" Reese asked leaning back casually in his chair. He did this not because he felt casual, but because he understood the need to ease the intensity of the moment for his son. Zach glanced around the familiar office. There was not a scrap of clutter in sight. There was nothing personal, no nick-knacks, none of his many rewards, not even a family picture on the chance that it would distract a witness or endanger someone he loved.

"She's got a talent other kids don't have," Zach spoke softly, still unsure of how to proceed.

"Speed it up, Son. You are wasting time trying to break it to me gently," Reese pressed.

Nodding, Zach sat forward in his seat. "Dad, she has electricity in her. She can control it."

Frowning, Reese leaned forward once more, "What do you mean?"

"She can control electricity. Electronics, and…" Zach looked away at the window. "After 6 years you would think I would have come up with a decent way to explain it." He ran his hand over his face. "When she was three, her favorite toy ran out of batteries. One of those little dolls that laughs and such. She brought it to me and asked me to fix it. I took her out to the shop, set her up on the workbench, and unscrewed the cover."

"You are still giving me too many details, Zach. I'd love

to hear the whole story later. Right now, I need the facts. We can circle back to details later if needed."

Zach looked slightly annoyed. "Alright, I'll get to the point. I didn't have the batteries to fix the doll. I went inside to take one out of a less loved toy. When I got back, she was trying to put the old batteries back into the toy. I explained to her that it didn't work, but she was so determined that I helped her, thinking I would prove my point." Zach looked his dad in the eyes. "Dad, the batteries worked. The old ones. She was only three, and somehow she produced electricity and charged those batteries."

Reese searched his son's eyes for any sign of a joke. Zach was dead serious.

"Zach, do you think this is why she was kidnapped?"

"I think it has something to do with this power she has, but I don't know." Standing, Zach paced the small room in an attempt to still his agitated emotions.

Reese scribbled something down and met Zach's eyes once more. "Am I correct in assuming that Valarie can do more than charge batteries now?"

———

"Seriously?! This is like the tenth red light in a row!"

Valarie's kidnapper was young and nervous. She guessed he was somewhere around 20 years old. His fingers tapped impatiently on the steering wheel as he glanced around the intersection. "Come on," he muttered, raking his fingers through his disheveled brown hair. He looked as if he had worn the same t-shirt and loose jeans for several days in a row.

Valarie studied him, trying to remember every detail so she could tell the police later.

"They said it would take five minutes." He pulled out his phone and unlocked it. A GPS map was open. He studied it, not realizing that Valarie could also see the screen. She could tell it was his first kidnapping. He turned off the screen and looked up at the traffic light, it was still red.

His eyes moved to the rearview mirror. Valarie could not decide if they were green or blue. She met his curious look with her own challenging stare as he studied his captive who sat with her arms crossed, stewing in the back seat.

"You are doing this aren't you?" he gestured at the red light.

She looked shocked, "You are blaming your incredibly bad luck on me?" She pursed her lips angrily. "Take me home."

He turned in the driver's seat to face her. "I have lived here for five years. Never in all that time have I gotten ten red lights on this street."

"Take me home," Valarie repeated. Her hands were tied together with a strip of cloth but she tried the door handle again. Child lock was still on.

He rolled his eyes. "Can't you at lease think of a different way to ask? I'm not taking you home, so stop repeating your worthless command. I was hired to get you. It is nothing personal, I just really need the money right now."

"So you got me, now take me home."

Her captor groaned and turned back to the road ahead. "This was supposed to be a ten minute job."

The light turned green and two cars made it through before it was red again.

"Now what was that?" He put his hand on top of his head as if it were going to blow. "That light was green for like five seconds. Three if you count the brief yellow light. This thing is messed up."

A car behind them honked, and nine-year-old Valarie had to smile.

He rolled down the window and leaned out to shout at the offending driver, "Keep your shirt on, Buddy. We are all stuck at this busted light."

"Help! Help! I've been kidnapped!" Valarie screamed as

he frantically groped for the button to roll up the window.

He glared at her, "What was that? Seriously? I've had it up to here with you." He leveled his hand just under his eyes.

"Looks like you've still got a few inches to spare," Valarie observed with a saucy air. "Take me home."

He let his breath out in an exasperated sigh. "I did not sign up for this."

"You are officially a kidnapper," Valarie pointed out. "Which means, when you forced me into your car, you signed up for a good stretch of jail time. I would say five to ten years at least. I don't know if I should point this out again, but my grandpa is Reese Calgen, the famous detective who has never had a case he couldn't crack. I would suggest, if you want to get that sentence shortened a few years, that you…"

"Take you home," he groaned. "Why does everything you say have to include that?"

He saw her eyes look to the side and a smug smile appear. He looked the direction her dark eyes had gone. Several police with their lights on were approaching the intersection. "Unbelievable."

They fanned out to each corner of the intersection. Valarie saw her captor relax visibly, "It is because the light is out, Sedge. Just stay calm."

"Sedge, huh? Take me home, Sedge." Valarie knew as soon as she said it, that she had gone too far.

His face grew dark with anger. How could he have been stupid enough to say his own name? He jerked around to face her once more. "Look, I don't know how you did the light thing, but you had better keep in mind I still have the gun. They said they wanted you alive, but if I have to use it, I will. You lay down on that seat and keep quiet."

The belligerent front she had been putting on vanished instantly, and he saw her for the young, fearful girl she was. She lay down and was quiet.

One cruiser pulled off the road onto the median, while another pulled off the road near the control box. The officer got out and opened the metal door. After a minute, he shook his head at the officer on the median, and spoke into his radio. The officer on the median got out of his car, tugging on a reflective safety vest as he made his way into the intersection.

Sedge looked back at her once more. Her thick, dark hair was held back by a bright yellow cloth headband that matched the shirt she wore. The smiling sunflower on the front of her shirt seemed out of place as she cowered against the seat. Her eyes were closed and her tied hands were folded together. It suddenly occurred to Sedge that she could be praying. The last thing he needed was God to intervene. He just needed the money. The bills were coming in faster than he could cover them. A quick job. That is all it was supposed to be. They promised they only wanted to ask her some questions. Nothing violent.

A sharp whistle drew his attention back to the street. The officer was waving him forward.

Sedge raised his hand in a "thank you/I'm sorry" gesture as he pulled across the intersection. The officer was watching Sedge's car. He looked puzzled. The kidnapper glanced at the back seat. The girl had not moved.

In his rearview mirror, Sedge saw the officer say something into his radio.

Panic welled up inside him, and Sedge hit the gas. He heard Valarie gasp in fear behind him.

He knew what she would have said. "Please take me home." But it was too late for that now.

CHAPTER 7

"Mr. Calgen, something is on channel 14.

Reese reached over to turn up his police scanner. A garbled voice came from the scanner.

The chatter was hard to discern, and Zach looked at his dad desperately "Is it her?"

Reese smiled, "After what you just told me, I think we have our suspect." He rose and checked his pocket for his keys and badge as he relayed the radio message. "An officer just reported a car that has all of its exterior lights flashing SOS, passing through an intersection where the traffic lights are acting up. We will head that way." Reese retrieved his Glock from his desk and slid it into his shoulder holster. "I wish you had trusted me with this sooner, Zach."

Zach was used to hearing disappointment in his dad's voice, but the sight of the gun rattled him. "Dad you don't think you will need that, do you?" Zach protested fearfully.

"I'm sorry, Zach. I do not know what to expect, but I have to be ready." He slipped into his suit coat, buttoning the top button without looking at it. "Let's go."

The elevator seemed to take forever as they descended the three floors to the ground level. Reese did not chide his son for his impatience. They strode quickly through the lobby to Zach's car which was parked outside. An officer stood with a paper in hand by the driver's door.

"Pete, you can give that to Nina, and I'll pay for it." Reese never slowed his stride as he approached the car.

Zach was amazed to see the officer nod and step away from the illegally parked car.

"Be safe out there, Calgen."

"I'll do what I can," Reese responded.

Zach slipped into the driver's seat, wondering how often these two men had exchanged the same words. They both worked jobs with no guarantee that they would survive the day. As Zach pulled away from the curb, he wondered if his dad had concealed the dangers he had faced in the same way Zach had concealed Valarie's strengths. Both men were opening up only as much as was necessary to get by.

"We will need my car," Reese informed him.

Zach turned sharply into the parking lot entrance and pulled to a stop on the yellow lines marking a no parking area. He would deal with that later. They scrambled from the car and slipped into Reese's grey Toyota Camry. The police knew Detective Calgen. They would be able to get right into the action if they had the right clearance.

Reese pulled out into traffic and flipped on his concealed lights and siren. This was his favorite gift from the police force. He used them sparingly so that the chief of police would not revoke his privilege. They flew down the road as traffic cleared before them. Zach looked over at his dad, studying the firm determined features. Reese's thick, tight curls were graying at the temples, but he worked hard to keep himself in good physical condition. His theory was, if you quit moving, you quit working. After years of people investing in him, Reese was determined to make a difference for others as long as he could.

"There they are," Zach pointed out. "This is only about half way across town from where he picked her up." Zach observed with a frown. "We called the police more than half an hour ago. Why would he stay around here?"

"I don't think he had a choice," Reese observed stepping out of the car. He showed his badge to the officer who came towards them to ask them to leave. The officer nodded and pointed out the car. A young man was up against the car, and an officer was patting him down.

"Valarie!" Zach ran forward only to be stopped by a young, police woman. "That's my daughter," Zach informed her.

"I'm sorry sir, I'm going to have to ask you…"

"Ma'am, he is with me," Reese interrupted, showing her his badge. She stepped aside reluctantly. "Stay out of the officer's way," she instructed, looking at Zach. "They are trying to do their jobs."

Zach sprinted across the road as Valarie was being helped from the car.

"Daddy!" Valarie's face puckered up and tears began to flow down her cheeks.

Zach enveloped her in his arms and held her tightly. He looked across the car at the young man who had forced his daughter at gunpoint into his car. He saw a defiant, older teen who was angry but compliant as the officers cuffed his hands behind him.

Reese on the other hand, saw a hopeless young man, angry at himself for what he had done. He knew this young man was about to face hours of interrogations about his motives and intentions. Reese estimated the kidnapper would get five years for this one-time fling unless he got out early on good behavior.

"You alright, Val?" Reese asked turning his attention to Valarie.

She nodded without taking her face from where it was hidden against her dad.

An officer knelt beside her. "Sweetheart, I'm going to free your hands. It might tug a little." He cut the cloth with blunt tipped scissors and gently unwrapped her wrists. She pulled her arms in close to her body and was content to remain cocooned in Zach's arms.

Reese extended his hand to the officer, "Thank you for what you did for my granddaughter."

The officer stood and shook his hand warmly. "This is the ending we were all hoping for."

"Reese Calgen."

"Trice Higgins."

They released each other's hands and surveyed the scene. The kidnapper was now seated inside a police car, his head resting on the back of the seat in front of him. The media swarmed for pictures and footage, each trying to get the best shot for their respective channels.

"They said on the radio that the kidnapper's lights were blinking an SOS signal," Reese observed casually.

Trice nodded. He was assigned to Valarie until the kidnapper was taken from the scene, and he was happy to talk while he waited. "It was the strangest thing. We got calls from multiple drivers reporting the lights at 12th and Dewey were out. When we arrived on scene, it didn't take long to spot this guy flashing his headlights and break lights for all he was worth. I've never seen something like that. Then, when he saw us coming, he made a run for it. Didn't make any sense at all. Maybe one of those mental issues where people have two personalities. Or a strange battle of his conscience. I'm glad I don't have the job of questioning these crazies."

The cruiser with Sedge inside pulled away and the all clear came over the radio.

"It's Valarie, right?" Trice asked Reese softly.

Reese nodded.

Trice lowered himself to one knee a little way from Valarie. She had stopped crying. "Valarie, we are going take a little ride to the hospital. Your Dad will come along. They just need to check you out and make sure you are okay."

"I'm okay." She turned so she could see him, and Trice offered her a pack of tissues. She sniffed and took it gratefully. Trice gave her time to blow her nose and wipe her eyes.

"You look okay, but we have to be sure. Do you want to ride in the ambulance? They brought one just for you."

"Ambulances are really expensive," Valarie answered softly. "Can I ride with my dad?"

Trice glanced up at Zach with a grin. "They are expensive, but sometimes they can save people's lives, and that is worth more than money."

"I know. But I don't want to ride in it."

"That's okay. I can tell them we do not need it." Trice caught the attention of one of the waiting paramedics and shook his head. She acknowledged his message with a quick nod, and her team started loading up the gurney they had ready.

"If you think you feel okay, we can all ride in my police car," Trice offered. Seeing no excitement in Valarie's expression, he gave her one more option. "Or we can ride with your dad, if you would rather."

"I want to ride with my dad."

"Let's do that then," Trice agreed. "Would it be okay if I ride with you? I get to ride in police cars all the time, but riding with a dad is pretty special."

Valarie nodded and sniffed in a shaky breath.

Trice touched base with his partner and gave him the keys to their cruiser before joining the Calgens once more. "Thanks for waiting. Let's get this hospital business out of the way so you can all go home."

CHAPTER 8

"Why did you kidnap Valarie?" the officer asked.

Sedge sat with his elbows on the interrogation table and the palms of his cuffed hands against his forehead. The tips of his fingers were hidden in his disheveled brown hair.

"I told you, a guy offered to pay me $1,000 for bringing her to him." The irritation left Sedge's voice as he added, "He said he wasn't going to hurt her."

"And you believed him?"

"I needed the money. It was either take a chance or get kicked out on the street."

"So you took a chance with a little girl's life?"

Sedge did not answer.

"Sedgwick, surely you can see that endangering the life of a nine-year-old girl for the promise of money was a really stupid thing to do."

"Look, I was desperate. I didn't think it through. He didn't seem like a bad guy, just wanted to ask her questions or something."

"Unbelievable."

Sedge dropped his hands and sat back in the chair. "I guess everyone was right. I'm just worthless. The only choices I make are dumb ones. It doesn't matter how much I try."

"You are not the victim here, Sedge," the officer spoke firmly and without compassion. "We are not even going to start down that road. I want you to think back to when you were at the malfunctioning light. In the intersection, you were flashing your lights in an SOS pattern. Yet when the officers came to help you, you gunned it and fled. Can you tell me what you were thinking?"

"So she did my lights too," Sedge muttered under his breath. Suddenly the pieces came together. The girl had some kind of super power, and these guys were out to get her. It was like a movie plot only instead of watching, Sedge found himself stuck in the middle of it all. He remembered her cowering against the seat and knew he would have to take the rap to protect her.

"What did you say?" the officer pressed.

"I didn't know my lights were flashing," Sedge told him honestly. "The intersection ones were messed up too. There must have been some kind of electrical wave or imbalance because I was not flashing my lights."

"We have footage of it."

"I am not denying they were flashing," Sedge paused to calm himself. "I'm saying I was not the one doing it." This was a lot bigger than he could have imagined. The man said he had a few questions for the girl. Now Sedge understood, and he had some questions himself.

"What does that mean? The girl was tied up in the back seat, and you were the only other person in the car. Who was doing it if it was not you?"

A shrug was the only answer he got.

The officer looked irritated. "Well, at least one of your worries is over. When your trial is over, you won't have to worry about housing payments for a long time."

———

"Grandpa?"

Reese looked up to see a dark figure standing in the door of the guest room. It had been late by the time they had gotten the clearance to go home after the kidnapping, and Zach and Brook had insisted that he stay the night in their guest room.

"Valarie? What are you doing up so early?"

"Can I come in?"

Reese smiled, "Of course, you can."

Her bare feet were silent on the thick carpet. She came to the recliner where he was and leaned against the thick arm of the chair. Her eyes fell on the Bible that was open on his lap.

"It was here, and I didn't have anything better to do." He seemed embarrassed to have been caught with the book. Closing it, he set it back onto the side table and gave her his full attention. "What is on your mind?"

"It will help you," Valarie told him seriously.

"What will?" Reese asked with a confused frown.

Valarie rubbed her eye sleepily. "The Bible. It has the words of life."

Reese patted her hand, "That is not why you came in here, is it? What did you need?"

"Why did Sedge kidnap me, Grandpa?"

"I don't know, Valerie. The police are trying to figure that out."

She stood quiet and thoughtful.

When she did not speak, Reese asked, "Was he rough with you?"

Valarie leaned her head against the padded side of the recliner, "No. He was scared when the police came, and yelled at me to get down and be quiet. He wasn't mean, just scared like me."

"Did he say why he kidnapped you?"

"He didn't say much at first. Later, he told me that he needed money."

"Hmm."

They drifted into a thoughtful silence.

"Grandpa?" Her voice sounded sleepy.

"Hmm?"

"Do you think I'm a freak?"

Reese turned to look at her.

"Who told you that?"

Valarie looked away, fingering the end of her braid. "A kid at the park, and Trent before Dad threatened him with the dreaded chore list." She smiled a little at the memory.

"Do the kids around here know about your power?"

"Not really. Dad said I shouldn't tell people because it might put me in danger. He said there are a lot of ways to use my power to help people. But I don't know what they are." She moved to look at him, her eyes innocent and questioning.

"Valarie, you are not a freak," Reese informed her firmly. "Your dad says all the time that nothing is made or given without purpose. You know that. Your gift was given to you for a specific reason. We do not know why yet, but we will."

Valarie threw her arms around him and hugged him tightly. "Thank you, Grandpa."

Without another word, she slipped out of the room as quietly as she had come.

———

"Dad? Dad! You gotta get up." Valarie's voice was slowly increasing in volume. "I have to go to the hospital."

Brook was instantly awake, "Valarie? What's wrong? Are you sick?"

"No, Mom, I'm fine. God said I need to go. They need me."

A clap of thunder startled them all. Rain poured down on the roof above them, making it hard to hear.

Zach sat up and blinked at the clock on the dresser. "Val, its 3am. Nobody will be up. The hospital isn't even open."

"Please Dad. It's important." She handed him the pants that had been folded over the back of the chair. "I can stay in my gym shorts," Zach protested with a yawn. "They aren't going let us in."

"Zach, I think you need to go with her." Brook sat up in bed to examine her twelve-year-old in the dim lamplight. She was wearing a water resistant jacket, snow pants, and boots. "Did you dig all that out of the winter bin in the garage?" When Valarie didn't answer, she asked, "You sure you feel okay?"

"I'm fine, Mom, really."

Thunder rumbled again.

"Please hurry, Dad. I had a dream, and if I don't get there in time, it will be too late."

"What will be too late?" Brook asked.

Zach emerged from the bathroom. He had changed into the pants but still wearing a worn t-shirt. Lightening lit the room as Zach crammed his bare feet into his tennis shoes. "Alright, let's go."

Valarie darted from the room, and Zach hurried after her.

"Be careful," Brook called softly after them.

Grabbing the key from the hooks by the door, Valarie hit the unlock button, cinched her hood tightly around her face, and ran out into the rain. Zach knew an umbrella would only slow them down, so he followed. The rain came down like a waterfall and he was drenched after the short sprint to the car.

Valarie put the key into her dad's hand. He started the car. The air turned off and the wipers turned on high without him touching either switch.

"You let me drive," Zach instructed pulling out into the empty street.

"Sorry, Dad. Please hurry."

He brought the car up to speed before glancing at Valarie. She had removed her hood and was sitting forward in her seat, chewing her bottom lip nervously.

"Why don't you pray?"

"God, help it hold until I get there," Valarie said aloud. It was a desperate, sincere prayer.

Zach glanced at her again. She was tense and trembling. "Can you tell me what is going on?"

"The power at the hospital can't hold up against this storm." She kept her eyes on the road. "The second generator is down. I saw the surge that took it out in my dream. One generator cannot create enough power to run the hospital."

The light turned yellow, flashed red, and was green again before Zach could slow down.

"Wow." He sped up, squinting to see through the deluge.

"Turn here," Valarie instructed confidently.

Zach obeyed.

She was scanning the road. Through the rain, they could see the lights of the hospital building to their right.

"Not this entrance, the little one up there, by the bike rack." She pulled her hood up and cinched the string once more.

He did not question her. Pulling in, he reached for the key. Lightening flashed brightly, illuminating a service door with a key card box mounted on the wall beside it. Zach instantly knew what she was planning to do. She was out before he could turn off the car.

"Valarie, wait." A boom of thunder drowned out his call.

She ran ahead through the blinding rain to the door. The card reader flashed green, and she disappeared inside. The door clicked shut before he could reach it. "Valarie?" He banged loudly, but she did not return. He stood in the rain, his hand on the handle of the door. He had to find another way in.

CHAPTER 9

Valarie raced through the basement. It was laid out exactly as it had been in her dream. She turned down a little hall and saw the high voltage room. She saw the card reader and powered its signal. It flashed green. Grabbing the heavy door, Valarie used her foot against the frame to pull it open leaving a wet shoe print on the gray metal. Going inside, she allowed the door to close behind her. The dim light above her clicked on. Shedding her jacket, snow pants, and boots, Valarie was careful not to step in the puddle they created. Throwing her things into a corner where they would be out of the way, she wiped her face on her sleeve, and her damp hands on her pants. Water carried electricity. This was more power than she had ever made, and she was not going to take any chances. Her dry socks made no sound as she went to the generator. There was just enough room to squeeze herself between the edge of the huge generator and the cement wall. Making electricity was like doing a plank and thinking very hard at the same time. Valarie knew it would be tiring. The wall would help her stay upright so she could concentrate on powering the damaged generator.

Taking a deep breath, she moved herself into position. The firm wall was comforting against her back. There was only an inch or two between herself and the huge generator.

Closing her eyes, Valarie laid her forehead against the cold metal and concentrated. The generator sputtered and the lights flickered for an instant. Valarie prayed hard, feeding the machine more and more power. With a roar it came to life. Valarie held it there.

———

"I tell you she's in there!" Zach moaned dropping into one of the plastic padded hospital chairs. He had tried every service entrance and was soaked through.

"And I tell you no one is in the basement." The security officer told him. "That is a restricted area. There is no way your daughter can be in there. You have to have a keycard or code to access that area." He jerked his thumb at the big grey door.

On the door, in neat block letters were painted the words, 'Authorized Personnel Only'.

"So what am I supposed to do?" Zach asked wearily. "It's been over an hour."

The officer caught the look of pity from the night nurse behind the counter. They had both dealt with drunks before.

"I would suggest that you go home and take a nice, hot shower."

"You don't understand." Zach stood up. "How can I make you understand that I need to get to my daughter?"

———

"Experts are calling it a miracle." The news anchor's tie was slightly askew and his eyes looked tired.

Brook, watching from home, guessed he had been pulled out of bed to catch the story.

"The hospital's main power source was struck with lightening nearly three hours ago. Local authorities have confirmed that the hospital's second generator went down during the storm around 3:17 this morning, leaving countless lives hanging in the balance. The one remaining generator could not maintain the level of power required to keep the entire hospital going. And yet, miraculously, the badly damaged generator is still producing power. This means that the life-saving machines inside the hospital behind me are still running strong."

The camera panned to show several lit windows in the hospital that loomed above the trees behind them.

"Teams of electricians are working frantically to repair the damage caused by the power surge and get the main power back on. Stay tuned for updates as we follow the hospital miracle as it unfolds."

Brook muted the commercial and looked at her phone. There had been no news from Zach in over an hour. She knew who was behind the miraculous power. Sliding from her chair, Brook got on her knees. Valarie would need God's strength to hang on.

———

"It doesn't make any sense." The electrician stared into the open panel. "This thing is fried. Look at those melted wires." The hospital director moved forward to look where the electrician pointed. "There is no way this thing can make power."

"And yet it is," the director pointed out. He looked back at the group standing in the doorway. They were the core of the hospital staff, the decision makers. Everyone was seeing the same thing, but no one knew how to explain it.

"I ran a test, and as far as producing power, this generator is outperforming the one that was not damaged." The electrician scratched his head. "I've never seen anything like this in my life."

"Can you repair it?" a lady in a well-fitting business suit asked.

"Honestly, Ma'am, I'm afraid to touch it. If it can hold

until the main power is restored, no one up there will be in danger. If I try to repair it now, this phenomena might stop."

"Too many lives are at stake to try something risky like that," a lean man in scrubs confirmed. He had already worked a double-shift, and it was starting to show.

"Keep someone down here to monitor the generator." The hospital director checked his watch, "I have to give the press an update in five minutes. Whatever you do, don't mess with the miracle generator as long as it is running."

"Yes, Sir."

"The press will want to know how the repair is coming. What should I tell them?"

"My men are confident that it should be up and running within the next hour. If this one can hang on that long, there will be no interruption in the hospital's power."

"It has been going for four hours now." The director looked at his team. "If any of you believe in God, this would be a good time to start praying."

———

"Listen, my daughter is inside. I need to get in there." Zach sat flanked by two officers. A third stood a little ways from him blocking the door to the basement.

The Chief of Security stood over the disheveled dad. "Sir, you do not have clearance to be down here. My team and I have told you this way too many times tonight."

"I don't know how long she can hold up," Zach begged. "Don't you see? She is powering the generator."

"I see."

The officers looked at one another knowingly.

"You have been trying doors all over the hospital since 3:30 am," the Chief of Security pointed out. "We even have footage of you trying to break through a window. You have been warned and detained multiple times. You seem like a nice guy, and I don't want to have to take you in since it has been a long, tense night for us all. Why don't you let these officers take you home?"

"Because my daughter…"

"Is powering the building," the officer by the door interrupted. "Sir, have you been drinking?"

Zach groaned, "Stop asking me that. No, I have not been drinking. I haven't even had water."

"Take him home," the Chief of Security instructed.

The officers helped Zach to his feet.

"Listen, I'm letting you off easy. But if you show up here again, I'll have to book you."

CHAPTER 10

The electrician assigned to the generator room was bored. Thirty minutes had passed, and he was tired of sitting on the padded folding chair he had been given. He stood and stretched, something colorful behind the trash can in the corner caught his eye. He glanced at the generator. It had sputtered twice since he had taken up his post. The director had been notified that the generator might not hold much longer. It seemed steady now, so he went to investigate the bright blue cloth that had caught his eye. He pulled out a waterproof jacket, snow pants, and pair of snow boots. They were small enough to belong to a young teenage girl. Checking inside, he found the name Valarie written on the tag of the jacket. There was no other form of identification. It bothered him that they were still damp. The floor showed there had been a puddle around them that was slowly drying up. Whoever this Valarie was, she had come in with the storm last night.

"Valarie?" He called hesitantly. "Valarie, are you in here?" He thought the sound of the generator changed slightly.

He felt uneasy. The room suddenly seemed creepy, as if something, or someone, was watching him. It is just a kid. He told himself. No need to get worked up about a teenage girl without her snow clothes hiding in a room with a… he stopped himself.

"Valarie?" he called again. His voice was drowned out by the roar of the generator. Moving forward he peered around every object. Even those too small to hide someone big enough to fit the damp clothes. "I'm not here to hurt you. You can come out." He noticed for the first time that the far end of the generator did not touch the wall. Keeping his distance he moved parallel to the big machine towards the far wall.

"Valarie, are you..." he stopped short. There, between the wall and the generator was a willowy girl in her early teens. She was pale and seemed to have wilted there, the wall and the side of the machine held her mostly upright. Her eyes were closed and her faced looked pained.

"Oh no." He exclaimed, thinking she was dead. Mustering up his courage, he took a step towards her. "Are you Valarie?"

Her eyes fluttered open. "Yes," she answered weakly.

The generator sputtered, and she closed her eyes tightly, pressing her forehead against the warm metal. It steadied once more.

"I need water," she told him, her voice sounded strange even to herself.

"Oh, okay. I'll..." he looked around, "I'll be right back."

"Don't tell them I'm here," Valarie pleaded.

"Okay, sure." He backed away. "No, I won't." He ran for the door and let himself out. Taking a deep breath he glanced around the empty basement. "Where do I get water?"

"Zach?" Brook looked questioningly at the officer who had escorted her husband to the door. He released Zach's arm once he was over the threshold.

"Ma'am, is this your husband?"

"Yes." She looked at Zach who looked tired and defeated.

He dropped onto the couch wearily. "They won't let me get to her, Brook. She's in there making power for the whole blessed hospital, and they won't let me help her."

"He's been creeping all over the hospital trying to get

through doors that he should not be going through," the officer explained. "My supervisor was lenient and allowed him to go home. If he shows up on the hospital grounds again, we will have to arrest him."

"I understand."

"Ma'am, does he drink often?"

Zach let out an exasperated sigh.

"No, Sir." It was all so ridiculous and surreal that Brook couldn't help laughing. "He doesn't drink alcohol."

"Is there something I should know?" the officer asked, looking from Brook to Zach.

"My husband and daughter left at 3am this morning to save the hospital. The hospital generator that was fried by lightening has been miraculously running since 3:17. And now you bring back my husband accusing him of being drunk. It is all a bit much to take in this early in the morning," Brook explained. The laughter in her eyes faded, and she looked at him hard. "If you won't allow her dad to find her, I would advise you to call out the whole police force and locate my daughter within the next thirty minutes. If you don't, I will get involved."

He stepped back, "Yes, Ma'am."

Hurrying back to his car, he pulled out with a screech of tires.

Brook turned and smiled at Zach. "Hi, Honey."

Zach laughed, shaking his head in disbelief. "I should have called you hours ago."

———

"Here, I got a straw."

Valarie opened her eyes again.

"If you are making that run, will the water convey the electricity?"

"I don't know," she answered weakly, licking her dry lips.

"They are almost done with the repairs. I checked very quickly while I was getting the water. Do you want it?" He was holding it out to her.

"I can't risk it," she whispered. "Thank you. It will be nice to have when the power is back on."

His radio chirped, and he stepped away so he could hear it. "They are making the last connections now," he told her.

The hum of the generator changed to an unsteady choking.

He went down on one knee so he could look the wilting girl in the eye. "I don't know how you are doing this, Valarie, but you have saved so many lives today. Hang in there for a little while longer. They need you to hang on."

She turned away, her eyes closed tightly against the pain of exerting energy she no longer had.

"When you ride a bike up a hill, it is the place right before the summit that is the hardest," he told her gently. "Keep pushing forward. You are almost to the top."

The hum increased and steadied once more.

"You are doing it. You are almost there." There was static on the radio. "Not yet, Valarie, keep it going." He moved the radio to his mouth, "How much longer, Mike? We don't have much time."

"Two minutes max. Is everything okay down there, Amerigo? You sound like you are standing in the generator."

"Let me know the second it is up and running," Amerigo responded. He laid the radio aside. The descending sound of the generator powering down filled the room. "No, no, hang on. They need you for two more minutes." He grabbed her arm and shook her gently, her skin cool and clammy. "Valarie. Two more minutes.

She took a deep breath and let it out as if awakening. Up went the power once more, though Amerigo could tell by the sound of it that the generator was running on just above the minimum power required.

He took her hand and massaged it gently. Her fingers were swollen and cold.

"It is on!" The voice on the radio was accompanied by cheers and applause in the background.

"You did it." Amerigo reached in and pulled the limp girl from the narrow slot as the power left the generator.

Taking his work jacket off, he wrapped it around her. Her clothes were damp with sweat and her whole body trembled. He picked her up and was almost to the door when it burst open. Brook cried out, and Zach surged forward to take his limp daughter from the electrician. "Is she okay?"

One of the officers with them stepped away to radio for medical assistance.

"I don't know." The electrician had tears in his eyes. "What she did was amazing."

CHAPTER 11

"Hi Valarie," Jessie said shyly. Even close friends seem a little strange at first when they are in a hospital bed. Jessie stood awkwardly by the bed as Valarie turned her head to see her.

"Hi Jessie. Thank you for coming."

"How are you feeling? Your mom said you powered the whole hospital for five hours!"

Valarie laughed, "Mom's exaggerate sometimes. I only powered half of the hospital. The other generator was still working."

Jessie came closer and sat on the edge of the bed. "Still pretty impressive if you ask me. I don't think I can do anything but sleep for five hours. I can't even watch TV that long. The worst part is that I can't tell anyone!"

"Poor Jessie," smiled Valarie. "You've known for ages anyway."

"It wasn't this big before." Jessie was quickly warming up in the presence of her friend. "The news is calling it the hospital miracle. Your parents would not let anyone tell how it happened. You are like a superhero, Valarie. Swoop in, save the hospital, and swoop back out under the cloak of mystery."

"I don't seem to be doing so well at the swooping out part," Valarie observed wearily.

"How do you feel?" Jessie asked again, this time waiting for an answer.

"I'm really tired and ready to be home," Valarie answered honestly.

Jessie glanced around with only her eyes and leaned in close, "We could sneak out."

Valarie grinned at the thought. "I don't think I'll get very far today, Jessie. I feel like a cooked spaghetti noodle."

They giggled together at the thought.

Brook came in with a tray of food. "Hey, you two better not be planning to sneak out of here without me," she warned with a smile. They broke into fresh peals of laughter. "I should have known better than to send Jessie up here alone," she joked, relieved to see her daughter laughing again. Yesterday, they had carried her limp body up from the basement. Exhausted, Valarie had slept for hours while being closely monitored by the machines she herself had powered for five hours the day before. The doctors were hopeful, but could not promise a full recovery. Only the director of the hospital, their police escort, and the electrician from the basement knew what she had done. Honoring her parent's wishes for privacy, the hospital director had personally overseen the doctor assigned to her care. She was treated simply as an exhausted twelve-year-old brought in by her worried parents. They had spent a tense night together not knowing what the next day would hold.

Brook smiled, glad Jessie had come. Valarie's color was returning and her eyes sparkled again with fun.

Valarie let Jessie push the button to raise her to more of a sitting position. Once the pillows had been adjusted, Brook placed the tray on Valarie's lap. She took their hands and said a quick prayer of thanks before removing the plastic cover. "Dig in, this is the best hospital food you will find in this whole building."

Valarie handed a little plastic container to Jessie, "Mom got the pudding for you."

Jessie pulled her legs up to sit cross legged on the bed. "I love pudding!" She put a big spoonful into her mouth and looked around the room contentedly. A vase of flowers from Zach stood cheerily on top of the dresser, and Brook had brought the colorful blanket that covered Valarie from home. "This isn't so bad," she observed. "Maybe I'll power a hospital someday."

Valarie laughed and threw her napkin at Jessie. "You can take my place. I'm ready to go home!"

————

The sun shone down brightly on Valarie and Jessie who were swinging together on the playground near their house. Usually, they left the swings to the littler kids, but today they had the park all to themselves.

"It's beautiful today!" Gripping the chains with her arms fully extended, Valarie leaned back to enjoy the sun on her face.

"What do you think we will grow up to be, Valarie?" Jessie asked, pumping her legs to catch up with Valarie's swing.

Looking over at her friend, Valarie laughed. "That was random. I believe we will grow up to be ladies."

"That's not what I mean, and you know it," Jessie protested. "Don't you ever think about the future?"

"Sure, I do." Sitting up in her swing, Valarie frowned thoughtfully. "Why do you ask?"

"My mom heard from a friend that someone saw my dad somewhere west of here. In another state," Jessie answered. "I thought, when I was a kid, that we would always be a family. And I hoped, after the divorce, that he would come back, and we could be a family again."

Their swings slowed down. Valarie was silent, sharing Jessie's pain as only a true friend can.

"He was with another lady," Jessie added softly.

"Jessie, I'm sorry," Valarie let her shoes drag on the ground, not knowing what else to say.

Jessie stopped her swing and looked over at Valarie, "When we grow up, can we still be friends?" Jessie's eyes were moist. "Even if we get different jobs and move and stuff. Could we stay friends?"

Reaching out to her, Valarie hugged her, swing and all. "Of course we can, Jessie. You will always be my friend." Releasing her, Valarie looked into Jessie's eyes. "And if you ever try to go away and try to forget me, I'll track you to the end of the world, if I have to. And when I find you, I'll remind you that I was your best human friend when you were a kid, and that I plan on keeping that title."

Wiping away her tears, Jessie tried to laugh.

"And you do the same for me, Jessie," Valarie was serious. "Because if I ever stop talking to you, you will know that I've either lost my mind or I've been kidnapped again."

"Don't even joke about that, Valarie," Jessie scolded. "That was the worst day ever." She looked out over the empty playground thoughtfully. "You know," she said at length, "I'm kind of hungry. You want to go get something to eat?"

Valarie laughed at the abrupt subject change, "Yes I do! Come on, best friend, let's go raid our pantry!"

———

"Dad, can we stop at that gas station?"

There was a tenseness in her tone that caused Zach to glance over at Valarie. There was more to her question. He could see it in her face. Looking past the red light at the dimly lit station on the other side of the intersection, Zach tapped his fingers thoughtfully on the steering wheel. "Val, it's almost 10. It is very dark and that place isn't very well-lit. Could I get you something at another store?"

"It has to be there." She was chewing her lip nervously, her eyes locked on the gas station. Her breathing had changed to a controlled rhythm.

Their 3 am drive to the hospital came to mind, and Zach remembered all that had happened afterwards.

The light turned green, and she met his eyes. "Please, Dad. I don't know why, but I need to go there now."

"Only if I can come with you this time."

The car behind them beeped politely, and Zach steered the car across the intersection, "Deal?"

"Dad, I don't want you to get hurt."

He pulled into the gas station parking lot and turned off the car. Giving her his full attention, he squeezed her hand gently. "I feel the same way about you. Let me go with you, Valarie. I won't get in the way."

She nodded, knowing she did not have time to argue. Slipping out of the car, she shut her door gently.

Zach followed her example.

"Keep it chill," Valarie instructed strolling toward the dim store.

If the situation had been different, Zach would have laughed at his teenage daughter's instructions. But there was nothing funny about her vague directions tonight.

A bad light above the door flickered eerily as they approached. The hanging sign inside the door said 'Closed' in big bold letters. Zach did his best not to be obvious as he scanned the area. No one was in sight. He could see the cashier between the advertisements that were stuck all over the dirty glass windows of the convenience store. He looked nervous. Something or someone out of sight was holding his attention. Zach opened the door for Valarie out of habit. She instantly started babbling.

"Just a quick snack, Dad. Can I get a cappuccino too? I could really use some caffeine right now."

"I don't know how your mom would feel about you having

caffeine so late," Zach responded cheerfully, following her lead. "How about we stick to some snacks tonight."

"But can't I get a drink? I'm parched. It will be hours before we get home."

Zach felt a flash of cold fear. They were only ten minutes from their house. What did Valarie know about what was about to happen?

"Hold it." A man stepped from between the aisles with a gun in his hand. He was Zach's height but several pounds heavier. Though his face was covered with a ski mask, they could still see his hard, hateful eyes.

Valarie gave a little cry and clung to Zach's arm. Zach was subconsciously aware that this behavior was uncharacteristic for his daughter, but he did not have time to think about it. How could he have allowed her to convince him to walk into a dangerous situation unarmed? He should have asked her more questions.

"Drop your phones in that basket and get on the floor," the man ordered gesturing with his gun. "Over there."

Zach and Valarie obeyed and moved cautiously in the direction he had indicated. They found themselves looking into the scared faces of a young man, two teenage girls who looked similar enough to be his sisters, and an overweight middle-aged man wearing pajama pants. They were already seated on the dirty floor. Valarie sat with her back to the snacks that lined the aisle and Zach sat beside her.

"This is supposed to happen," Valarie whispered. "Be scared and dumb."

Their captor sent a bullet into the ceiling tiles. The teen girls gave stifled cries and everyone ducked, their eyes wide with fear.

"Keep quiet." He was glaring at Valarie.

She nodded silently. She did not have to pretend to be scared.

Jerking around to face the cashier, he waved his gun menacingly. "I thought you locked that door. You got that money out yet?" he demanded.

"Yeah, it's right here." The cashier looked young enough for this to be his first job. His hands trembled as he piled up the money on the counter.

"Put it in a bag, you moron," the man ordered, sending another bullet into the ceiling.

He glanced at his cowering prisoners with cruel enjoyment. "If you don't hurry up, I might start knocking off these witnesses. Who will be first? How about the blabbing girl wanting a little caffeine to stay awake? Are you awake now?"

Valarie nodded, wide-eyed.

"No, don't hurt them. I'm hurrying." The cashier was scrambling to put the money in a plastic sack. Dropping it on the floor in his haste, Valarie could see he was near the cracking point. Tears were starting as he madly crammed the wads of cash into the bag. She moved her hand slightly to touch her dad's, knowing he was about to leap into action. She felt him relax beside her. Neither dared to look at the other. All eyes were on the man with the gun.

Outside the lights over the pumps went out, flickered back on, and then went out again.

"What was that?" the man demanded.

"They are on a timer," the cashier explained. "I guess it's not working. I can turn them back on. They are supposed to be on all night."

"Shut your mouth," he was aiming the gun at the brown haired teen now. She put her hands over her mouth to keep from crying out, her face deathly pale.

Freezing where he was, the cashier clamped his mouth shut, drawing his lips in between his teeth.

"Forget about the lights and get the money or this girl will be the first to pay." His eyes scanned the shelf behind the attendant. "Add those lottery tickets too, and give me some cigarettes."

The cashier scrambled back behind the counter to obey.

Police lights flashed, filling the store for an instant. The next moment, it was dark again. The hostages glanced at each other to see if they had imagined it. Without looking, Zach knew Valarie was involved.

The robber went to the window, cursing angrily as he peered out into the darkness.

CHAPTER 12

"Are you mad?" the police officer hissed angrily at his partner. "What was the idea of flashing your lights, Finley?"

"I didn't flash them. They just flashed," Finley protested hotly.

"Well, however it happened, everyone inside knows we are here."

"We don't even know if anyone is inside." Peering through the windshield at the lit interior of the station's convenience store, Finley corrected himself. "I can see someone moving around by the counter, there are at least two people inside. Do you think there are hostages?"

"I wouldn't be surprised. These routine stops always blow up into something bigger."

"How do you think they flashed the pump lights like that? You know that's why I stopped."

"I don't know. I'll call for back up. You try to keep your cruiser lights from flashing again."

———

"You three, go to the back door and get out," Valarie hissed pointing at the three younger hostages. "Go now, and be quiet."

When the teen girls did not move, the young man got to his feet and peered over the aisle at their captor. His attention was still on the dark parking lot. Staying in a low crouch, the young man took the girls' arms and propelled them down the aisle. Once they were in motion, they fled softly together towards the back of the store.

The masked man turned at the sound of the scuffle, but the red and blue lights flashed again in the parking lot, drawing his attention back to the lot. He strained to see the police cars in the darkness. The unsettling flickering of light above the door continued.

Valarie pointed at the bigger man in pajama pants and motioned for him to slide around the end of the aisle. There was an ice cream chest freezer that might shield him from some bullets if it came to that. He scooted slowly, his flannel pants making no noise on the floor.

"I know they are out there," the robber muttered. He turned on the cashier who backed into a shelf, sending items crashing to the floor. "You called them didn't you?"

Valarie gave her dad a little shove, the masked man was still an aisle away. Zach moved quickly after the big man, and the three of them crouched behind the freezer.

"I didn't call them. I promise I didn't." The cashier was talking fast. "The button doesn't even work. The money is ready, and I put the other stuff in too. You can take anything, please don't hurt anyone."

"It's too late for that. You took too long." The robber was moving forward with the calculated movements of a killer.

The store lights went out, and the man's gun barked rapidly spraying bullets haphazardly around the store.

The front door jingled and the strong commanding voice of the police filled the store. The store lights came on again revealing the masked man who was in the process of ejecting his empty clip. He grabbed for the clip on his belt but the police were on him before he could reload.

"We can go now," Valarie whispered, touching her dad's arm. Staying low, she sprinted for the back door. Zach followed her without speaking.

Moments later, the masked man lay face down. Finley, his knee in the man's back, was cuffing his hands behind him while his partner removed the two ammo clips from the criminal's belt and retrieved the gun.

They rose, weapons drawn. "Anyone else here?"

"He was the only robber," the cashier rose slowly from behind the counter.

Finley moved forward and helped the trembling young man to sit on the floor. "Are you hurt?" he asked, standing once more so he could keep his partner in sight.

"No, just shaken up. He had some of my customers as hostages. They had to sit there while he waved his gun around and threatened us all. I was so scared, I kept dropping the money. I wasn't trying to mess things up."

Finley acknowledged his partner's all clear signal. "Trice, this guy mentioned hostages. You got anyone back there?"

"There's one man at the end of the aisle, here." Trice answered. "He's not hurt. Apparently, the others got out the back when your lights distracted the robber."

The cashier looked up at Finley with haunted eyes. "I know he would have killed them if the lights hadn't gone out. You guys got here just in time."

"I think there was something bigger than the police force at work tonight," Trice observed, going back to where their prisoner lay. He looked out into the darkness. "Backup should be here any minute."

———

"How did you do that?" Zach asked in awe once they had pulled into their driveway. Neither one of them had spoken since they had slipped out the back door of the gas station. Circling the station in a wide arch, Valarie had led them back to the car where they were able to make their getaway before the rest of the police arrived.

Valarie turned her head toward him without bothering to lift it from the headrest. "That was really scary, Dad."

Zach couldn't help laughing. "Scary? Valarie that was terrifying."

She grinned back, "You did good. We are a pretty crazy team, huh, Dad."

Rubbing his face with both hands, Zach looked over at her again. "I have a superhero for a daughter."

"It wasn't me, Dad. God told me what to do." Valarie sat up, grinning again. "I was scared stiff."

"It is comforting to know that I was not the only one." He reached over and laid his hand on her arm. "Honey, that was a tense situation. Are you okay? Like, for real?"

"We both might need a little counseling," Valarie answered, laying her head back again. "But I think I'm okay. She turned her head his way and met his eyes. "You?"

Shrugging, he stuck his bottom lip out. "Who me? I just walked into a hostage situation, almost had to watch my daughter get shot, and snuck out the back door. I have to be honest, Valarie, I'm a little shook up. You could have died."

"They all would have if we hadn't stopped."

The way she said it sent a fresh wave of emotion over Zach. He knew she was right. He took a deep breath and let it out slowly. "Valarie, your gift is incredible. But I want you to know that I love you so deeply, that if anything happened to you, a big piece of my heart would die forever."

"I know. I love you too, Dad."

"I really mean it." They said it at the same time and laughed.

Zach took her slender hand in his and squeezed it gently. "How can I help you with your gift?"

Unbuckling, Valarie shifted in her seat looking thoughtful. "I think I need to learn more about electricity. I know a little, but if I knew more about how things worked, I might be able to use it better or to do more."

"Funny you should mention that. A few weeks ago, an older gentleman gave me a brochure about an electricity class they are having at the college next semester." He opened the console between their seats and pulled out the brochure. Smoothing it out, he handed it to Valarie. "He said they were hoping to get some high school students in to give them a taste of the class. You know, trying to recruit people early for their college. Although you are younger than they were looking for, they might make an exception. I could ask, if you are interested. He said the class would be free."

Valarie was looking over the brochure. "I don't know if I could keep up with a college class."

"You? Valarie you are brilliant." Zach grinned at her. "They would be the ones trying to keep up with you."

CHAPTER 13

"Valarie Calgen?"

"Here."

The professor looked over his wire rimmed glasses at the new student. Satisfied, he looked back down at his roster. "Brent Starclish?"

"Here." The tall teen standing beside Valarie said in a bored tone. His light brown hair was gelled in a haphazard way, and his whole appearance proclaimed to the world that he did not care. Even his glasses were loose and sat crooked on the bridge of his nose. Valarie thought he looked older than the other students who stood in pairs behind the wheeled, wooden workbenches that formed a semi-circle around the professor's stand/sit desk.

"Have you taken this class before?" Valarie asked in a whisper.

He looked at her through his glasses with narrowed eyes. "Don't be a smart alec."

Valarie frowned. "I wasn't trying to be smart, Brent. This is my first time and I…"

"I'm not showing you the ropes or being your friend, kid. This class is tough stuff and you are what, twelve?" He looked at her dully. "Basic Electronics. It is not for you unless you are some kind of brain child. So get all the ideas of friendship out of your tiny head and pull your own weight. I'm only paired with you because of him," he grumbled gesturing at the teacher who was finishing up roll call.

"Oh, I'm sorry you got a lame partner." Valarie's tone was genuine and he glanced over at her with a hint of surprise. She made no effort to defend herself.

"Brent, thank you for filling in the new girl." The professor laid aside his attendance list and added, "Next time wait until after I have completed the roll."

A couple of teen girls who looked like they were used to pulling their own weight looked at Brent knowingly. Valarie noticed that their expressions were more condescending than friendly.

"Class, Valarie is a transfer student of sorts. She is thirteen and has been homeschooled until now."

The girls looked again, and Valarie wished she had the power of invisibility instead of electricity.

"Valarie has expressed interest in electricity and how it works." The professor continued, aware of the discomfort of his newest pupil. He himself was not a fan of a child joining his advanced class. "Her parents have obtained permission from the dean for her to enroll in this lab for the semester. If she can keep up, she will finish out the year and receive an honorary certificate of achievement."

When he had finished, Brent glanced over at Valarie who was blushing with embarrassment. "Ouch," he whispered.

She glanced at him briefly, and he could see she was about to cry.

He turned his attention to the items on the workbench they shared. "Don't do it. That is what they want. If you buckle they will never let you live it down," Brent informed her under his breath.

Stooping, Valarie pretended to be searching her bag for her text book. When she stood and set it on the bench, her face was controlled and pleasant once more.

Brent glanced at her and nodded. She had what it would

take.

———

"Jessie, how do you stand being in school?" Valarie asked, going out of her way to crunch the biggest dry fall leaves.

Jessie shrugged. "I never had a choice, Valarie. You know that."

"Sorry, it's just that the other girls in the class are such snobs. They won't even talk to me. I tried at first to be nice, but they ignore me or talk about me like I'm not there. It is so annoying."

"You are almost through the semester though. Just a month left, right?"

Valarie sighed. "Yes, and you are almost done too."

Grinning, Jessie jumped in front of Valarie to crunch a large, dry leaf. "Yes, I am!"

"That was mine." Valarie shoved her playfully.

Jessie turned suddenly to look into the window of a dusty, abandoned shop. There had been a fire in the roof a year ago, and no one had bothered to repair it. The scorched ceiling tiles were still hanging down into the main room. They had looked inside the tinted windows with interest after it happened, but now it held very little mystery and attracted even less attention.

"Valarie, that Asian professor guy is watching us again," Jessie hissed fearfully. "You got your bracelet on?"

"Yes." Valarie followed Jessie's example. Pretending to look into the window, she scanned the reflection of the street behind them. "Yeah, that's Dr. Nee alright. Did I tell you that he comes to my class sometimes to observe?"

Jessie nodded.

"It's like he found out we walk this way and comes at the same time on purpose." Valarie pointed out a hanging ceiling tile inside the damaged building to make their act more believable. "I catch him watching me in class too," she went on. "You know how some people can make you nervous without doing anything?"

"Yeah," Jessie whispered as if afraid he would hear her.

They watched in the reflection as the older man found his place on the bench and opened his newspaper. He glanced over the top of it at them.

"Should we call the police?" Jessie asked.

"He's sitting on a bench. I don't think that is illegal."

"Valarie, I get so scared." Jessie's face had gone pale, and she slipped her arm through Valarie's and held tightly to her friend. "I won't let them take you again."

"Stop it, Jessie. That old man couldn't take us anyway." Valarie said it, but she did not believe it. A gun in anyone's hands gave that person an unfair advantage. "Let's go, keep it casual," Valarie instructed, guiding Jessie down the sidewalk. The tall trees that loomed over them seemed suddenly ominous in their rustling. They walked for several minutes before a police car pulled up beside them.

"You alright?" The officer leaned forward to see them through the open passenger window.

"Hi Mr. Trice, I'm sorry to bother you."

"I would much rather come when you ping me than to search for you after something happened," Trice told her seriously. "Hop in. I'll take you home."

The girls scrambled into the back seat together.

"All set?" Trice asked them, checking the rearview mirror.

"Yes, thank you."

The officer's presence lifted their fears, making them giddy with relief. Jessie cracked a joke, and they struggled to suppress their laughter.

Trice understood the emotional release relief brought and gave them a minute to adjust. He pulled to a stop at a red light and spoke casually, "So, Valarie, tell me what was going on."

"That older man on the bench back there, Dr. Nee. He is somehow attached to the class I am taking at the college," Valarie said, the laughter gone from her eyes.

"He is a creeper, Mr. Trice," Jessie added. "He's always around, watching us. Like he is planning something."

"I know it isn't illegal to watch people or sit on benches, but there is something about the way he does it," Valarie explained. "I don't know if that makes sense or not. Maybe I'm just crazy. There is something about him that makes me uneasy."

"Don't you girls ever ignore that feeling," Trice told them seriously as he navigated the turn into the neighborhood. "That is given to you by God for your protection."

They were surprised by the intensity of the easygoing officer's tone. "Any time you sense that, you ping me. Got it?"

They nodded seriously.

"I'll see what I can find out about this Dr. Nee. I think I know of a detective that might be able to lend his services."

Valarie grinned. Her grandpa was retired now, but he was always ready to offer his skills to help out the police force.

Trice got out and opened the side door for them.

"Here you are. Give me the wave if it is all clear inside."

Grabbing their book bags, they clambered out of the car. After thanking him, they hurried inside.

A minute later, Valarie waved from the kitchen window. Trice waved back and pulled away from the curb.

Across the street, a man stood on the sidewalk, letting his dog smell something in the grass. He was well built and alert. Valarie had never seen him before. Something about him wasn't right. He was watching their house, unmindful of the dog at his feet. Valarie wondered if the animal was a cover, a prop to allow him to observe their house unnoticed. His eyes met Valarie's, and she moved away from the window

with a twinge of fear.

CHAPTER 14

"Dr. Nee? May I have a few minutes of your time?" Zach Calgen stood by the public bench where the older man was seated.

Laying aside his book, Dr. Nee gave Zach his full attention. "Of course, sit down."

Zach sat out of politeness.

"How can I help you, Mr. Calgen?" Dr. Nee asked.

"My daughter Valarie is in an electronics class at the college that you are somehow connected with."

The Asian professor smiled pleasantly, "You will be happy to know she is doing very well."

"That is not why I found you." Zach's serious tone produced a confused frown on the professor's face. "Valarie has complained that you have been tailing her."

"Tailing?"

"Following her, watching her," Zach explained. "You may not have heard, but about four years ago Valarie was kidnapped."

The look on Dr. Nee's face was not one of surprise. Zach thought the expression was something closer to regret. He eyed the professor warily. "That type of trauma has a lasting effect on a person, especially a child."

"It must have been terrible for her," Dr. Nee responded sympathetically.

"It was. You can understand why I, as her dad, am very

protective of her. And will do anything to ensure her safety."

"What can I do to help?"

Zach looked intently at Dr. Nee. "I need you to stop watching her."

Dr. Nee blinked in surprised.

"Stop following her. Stop observing her. Find another bench to read on after school hours."

"It is a public bench, Mr. Calgen. I am not here to watch your daughter." Something about the way he said it caused Zach to doubt the man's words.

"Would you swear to that in court?" Zach's gaze was unwavering.

Dr. Nee's eyebrows went up. He tried to respond but could find no words.

"Dr. Nee, I will give my life to protect my daughter. I am asking you to respect her privacy and give her space to live without fear. If that means finding another time to read, or doing it on another bench, I think we can agree that her protection would be worth a little inconvenience." Zach stood and looked down at the stunned man. "And don't hang around her workbench in class. Around here, people get picked up by the police for things like that."

———

"Your dad really talked to him?" Jessie asked peering over the side of the bed.

Valarie, who was sprawled on the floor beside her book bag, nodded in amazement.

"I wish I could have been there!" Pulling a sour gummy worm from the package on the bed beside her, Jessie popped it into her mouth.

"Oo, me!" Valarie opened her mouth and closed her eyes tightly.

Jessie tossed a worm her way. The candy missed her

mouth, sending grains of sugar across Valarie's face.

"That was a terrible throw," Valarie laughed. She sat up to wipe the sugar away before retrieving the gummy worm and popping it into her mouth.

"It is all in the catch on these things." Jessie tossed a worm up and caught it on the first try. "You have to practice if you want to be as good as me."

"Is that how it works?" Valarie grinned. She lay back on the floor again, chewing contentedly. "Jessie?"

"Hmm?"

"Thanks for not being one of those boring friends who only talks about boys and stuff like that. Some of the girls in my class are ridiculously boring."

"Still not talking to you?"

"Not unless I do something dumb," Valarie answered in irritation.

Jessie folded her hands under her chin on the side of the bed and looked down at her friend. "How's that big electricity project coming along?"

"It's not that big of a project. All we have to do is make a lamp that works. It is kind of lame for an electronics class." Valarie squinted up at Jessie and dimmed the ceiling light slightly so she could see her better. "You would think they would have us actually wire something like a circuit board or create some kind of electronic device."

"You did say that this is only the second year this class was offered," Jessie pointed out. "And you already wired like twenty other complicated things. Maybe they wanted everyone to pass so the class would look good."

"Maybe so. The wiring is easy. Making the lamp worth looking at is another thing all together. Thankfully Brent, my bench partner, has a dad who used to do woodworking. He used his dad's tools and came up with a cool, rustic design. I'll stain the pieces and we will run the one wire and finish

it up in class. He should have taken woodworking or something hands on like that instead of electronics. But I think
he's at least up with the rest of the class now."

"Thanks to you," Jessie pointed out.

Valarie grinned. "I'd say he's shaping up nicely after a few
good pep talks and a ton of extra study. He was dragging his
feet in every class before. I can see why he was held back.
Now, he might even make something of himself someday."

Valarie put her hand up, and Jessie deposited a piece of
candy in her palm. "You want to know something really odd?"

"Of course." Jessie helped herself to another gummy worm.

"So I might have been snooping just a little," Valarie said
around the candy in her mouth. "But I saw Brent go into
that little coffee shop on the edge of the main building. You
know the one where we got that nasty drink that one time?"

"How could I forget that? That was the day we decided
that we were more of the ice cream type."

"Right. Anyway, there are two ways in, one through the
college and the other out front."

"So far, nothing is odd or new," Jessie pointed out.

"I usually leave right after class, but one day I stayed to
ask the professor about Dr. Nee hanging around and all."

"Before your dad talked to him."

"Right. Anyway, I saw Brent go into the coffee shop
through the college hall entrance. A few minutes later, a guy
the same height goes out the outside exit."

"Was it him?"

"I think it might have been. But he looked totally different. You know how I told you he always wears lame clothes
that look kind of frumpy?"

"Yeah?" Jessie propped her elbows on the bed and rested
her chin on her palms.

"Well, the guy who left was wearing a really sharp outfit.
His clothes could have been tailored specifically for him.

He didn't have his glasses and his hair was, well," Valarie searched for the right way to describe it. "I don't know, he looked professional."

"That's super odd," Jessie agreed. "Did you ask him about it?"

Valarie laughed. "No, what am I going to say? Hey Brent, usually you look like a slob who doesn't care, but this one day I was stalking you after class, and you actually looked kind of sharp. What's up?"

"Then you would be the odd one!" Jessie laughed. "But you only have a week left to find out. You are still planning on doing classes online and clepping classes next semester, right?"

"I think so. That class was enough to get my feet wet, as Dad puts it. I will do as many classes online as I can. They waste so much time in class."

"Welcome to my world," Jessie groaned. "Some of us don't have a choice."

Valarie brightened the light above Jessie and sat up. "Why couldn't we study and do it together?"

"Because," Jessie pushed herself up to sit cross-legged on the bed. "I'm a year younger than you and not half as smart."

"That's not true!" Valarie jumped to her feet and grabbed a pillow from the bed to whack Jessie with. "Take it back, Jessie, or suffer my wrath!"

At that moment, Brook's voice came from the kitchen, "Jessie, your mom is here."

Jessie leapt from the bed with a triumphant laugh and darted from the room. "See ya later, smarty pants!"

Chapter 15

Zach came into the living room and noticed Valarie sitting alone on the couch. "You okay, Val?"

She nodded, unconvincingly.

"No sign of Dr. Nee, or the 'Watching Dog Man' as you so fittingly have named him?" He said it lightly, but Valarie knew by his expression that he was ready to drop everything to keep her out of harm's way.

"No, not since that day when Mr. Trice dropped us off." Valarie shivered, "That was really creepy."

"That's good."

"Mom said you talked to Dr. Nee last week."

"I may have stepped in." Zach did his best to look innocent.

"Thanks for caring, Dad." Valarie was rewarded by a proud look of satisfaction.

"Enough about me. What's behind that somber look you are wearing?" He crossed the room and sat on the couch beside her. "Anything I can help with?"

She heaved a sigh. Pulling up her knees, she leaned against him. "This electricity class is annoying."

"Because of the content, or the classmates?"

Looking up at him with a smile, she said, "Grandpa would have asked that." She saw her dad's face cloud and wished she had not said it. Looking down at her knees, she asked, "Do you think you will ever be able to forgive Grandpa for being busy, and putting work first when you were a kid?"

"You have been talking to your mom about me, I see." Zach put his arm around her. His eyes were on the empty chair across the living room, but his thoughts were somewhere else. "I need to," he said after a long pause. Shaking his head he bit his bottom lip. "I try to Valarie, I really do. I think I've got it down, and then the smallest things make me flare up again. The hurt won't go away."

"I don't think it ever does."

He looked down at her, waiting for her to go on.

"I've talked to Mom about it a lot. Not about you," she clarified, "about forgiving. Sedge kidnapped me almost five years ago, and I still think about it sometimes. Actually, I think about it a lot. I was really scared, Dad." She leaned in closer to him. "The hurt of that doesn't go away. But I have decided to forgive him. Mom said if I ask God to help me, and decide to forgive him, it is done. My angry feelings still come sometimes, but instead of thinking about what he did, I pray for him and remind myself that I already forgave him. When I started praying for him, God slowly changed my heart. I still feel scared sometimes, and I don't understand why it had to happen. But I'm not mad at him for what he did anymore. I honestly want God to help him."

Zach was quiet for a long time.

"It is hard because of the other students," Valarie finally said softly.

"What?"

"You asked what made the class hard." She smiled up at him. "The content is very interesting, but the other kids, and the professor, don't like that I am there."

"Do you think it makes them feel dumb to have a kid who's not quite 14 acing their class?"

Valarie grinned. "I'm not acing it exactly."

"I could come give them a piece of my mind," Zach offered with a grin. He knew what her response would be.

"Dad." Valarie nudged him with her elbow, and he laughed.

"Keep in mind that I am here for you at the drop of a hat. You are my girl. If some people don't realize how special you are, I am happy to knock a little sense into them."

"Who are you knocking?" Trent asked, coming through on his way to the kitchen. "I could help."

"No one is knocking anyone," Valarie insisted with a laugh. "Especially not you two."

Trent looked at Zach and shrugged, "Females get so squeamish about these things."

"Hey!" Valarie threw the decorative pillow at him as he dashed from the room.

"If the class is too much for you, you will let us know, right?" Zach was serious again, and Valarie was grateful to know he would back her.

"I will. My bench partner is not very good at electronics or how things like that work. So I am learning a lot more by helping him to get it. I think he transferred from some other school and needed the extra credits because he failed a couple of classes last year and thought this class would be easy enough to pass. He's a year behind, and the other students give him a hard time about it. I've helped him catch up, and I think he's on track to graduate."

"How old is he?"

Valarie read the underlying question. "He's ancient, Dad. Like 20's at least."

"Twenty is not ancient!" Zach exclaimed. "What does that make me, young lady?"

"Pretty old I guess." Giggling, Valarie scrambled off the couch and out of reach. "I better go study. We have a big project." Valarie wiggled two fingers of each hand like quotation marks as she said it.

Zach laughed, "I thought you said it was a super simple lamp."

"It is. We have to assemble our lamp and have it ready and working by Thursday night."

"Only two days left." Zach leaned back into the couch. "You know, I could use a new lamp for my office back there. Mine has a bad bulb, and it is so ugly that I'd rather replace the whole thing. If your lamp works, and is manly enough, I might buy it from you. Then you can take me out to ice cream with the money."

"Deal." Valarie shook her dad's hand with a mock sober expression. "Brent already said lamps are old fashioned and that he doesn't want it. I'll bring it home Friday after class, and you can see what you think."

———

"It worked when we left, yesterday." Brent hissed, checking the power cord for the tenth time. He wore an obnoxious, orange button-up shirt that Valarie wished she had the power to dim.

"What could have happened?" Brent asked. He adjusted his glasses and stooped to test the outlet for power.

Valarie was frowning thoughtfully as she removed the wooden panel that concealed the inner wires of the lamp. She thought of the doll that had been her first glimpse into the world of electricity and smiled. Her dad would like this lamp if she could get it going again. It was shaped like a miniature old fashioned pump. The handle, attached to the pull string, turned it on when it was pushed down.

"Did you find out what is wrong?" Brent asked peering inside the wooden box.

"Yes I did." Valarie pulled the end of a cut wire out where he could see it.

"Someone cut it? Valarie, if I don't pass this class, I'm doomed. My dad won't pay for another semester. He's only paying half now."

"Calm down, we can fix it. Get me a wire nut, and don't draw a lot of attention to yourself."

Seeing she had a plan, Brent sauntered away to find what he needed on the supply shelf

"What's the matter, Brent, your project not working right?" A nerdy boy who got straight A's called loudly.

"Oh, um," Brent fumbled with the little plastic drawer he was sliding back in place, "Just cleaning up a few loose ends." Brent shot a perceptive glance at Valarie and saw Dr. Nee approaching their shared bench. Opening and shutting a few more drawers, Brent gave Dr. Nee a little extra time alone with Valarie.

CHAPTER 16

Brent was still searching for the wire nuts across the room when Valarie became aware of someone standing close to their bench. Their professor had started by the door and was slowly moving from bench to bench to observe and grade the projects. It would be several minutes before he reached them.

She glanced up to see Dr. Nee. He had visited their class several times early on in the semester.

Before her dad had spoken to him, the man had come often to observe the work of the students. This was the first time she had seen him since their talk. He stood across the bench from her, looking at her intently.

"You light it." Dr. Nee instructed. His eyes were alive with interest.

"Excuse me?" Valarie wished Brent would hurry.

"Light it. The professor will reach your table before your partner returns. This project is half of your grade. You cannot pass the class unless it works."

"I don't know what you are talking about, Dr. Nee." All at once she did. Somehow this man new about her gift. Valarie did not meet his eyes.

"You do know what I am suggesting," Dr. Nee countered. "I see it in your face. I know who you are, Valarie. You can light it and save your grade."

A cold tingling feeling of fear crept up her spine. She took a breath and calmed herself before turning to face him.

"No." Her tone was firm. She pasted on a smile as she continued. "The cord has been cut, Dr. Nee. If the circuit is not complete, the electrical current cannot reach the light bulb."

Raising her hand high she waited with her eyes on the professor.

"Don't be foolish, you don't have time to repair it," Dr. Nee pressed.

Brent moved between them, not appearing to notice Dr. Nee. "Here, the bin was empty but I scrounged around and found these two. It won't look nice, but it should work if we expose the wire first." Brent looked at her. "Why are you raising your hand?"

Across the room, the professor asked the same question.

"Professor, our lamp does not work because Dr. Nee cut our wires last night," Valarie spoke in a strong, clear voice.

Everyone blinked at her in surprise.

"We would like permission to repair our lamp before the final grade is given. I have pictures and video of the lamp working yesterday at the end of class. If you would like to examine it first, we should be able to use a wire nut to reconnect the damaged wire."

He had been coming toward her the whole time she spoke. "You have a lot of nerve accusing Dr. Nee of sabotaging your project, young lady," the professor hissed. Returning his voice to its normal level for the benefit of the class, he went on. "Dr. Nee is a major sponsor of this wing of the college, and this class would not be possible without his funding."

She looked at Dr. Nee, her expression knowing. "Thanks for the funding, Dr. Nee."

"Really, Valarie, I am shocked at your behavior. It is out of character for you to treat someone so coldly. Especially someone who made it possible for you to be here at all."

"So the brochures were from you?" Valarie eyed the short, graying man skeptically. "That's how my parents found out about it."

Brent leaned in, "Valarie, what are you doing? This class credit is important."

"Back to our project," Valarie transitioned smoothly. "You can see here that the wire was cut." She unlocked her phone and showed him the pictures of the lamp the day before. The professor declined her offer to show the videos. "Reconnect the wires. I will check your project last." He moved quickly to the next bench.

Valarie did not miss the displeasure on Dr. Nee's face.

They set to work and soon had their lamp reassembled. When the professor pressed down on the pump handle, the bulb lit instantly beneath the green shade.

He examined the inside, making no comment about the bright yellow wire nut. "Your project passes. Congratulations, Brent. Thanks to Valarie you might get enough credits to finish your degree." He turned to face the room. "Well done, class. You are free to leave after you have cleared off your benches. I will probably see some of you next semester."

"Ignore him, Brent," Valarie instructed, turning off their lamp. "You did as much on this project as I did."

"He's right though." Brent shoved his battered textbook into his backpack. "I wouldn't have passed without your help."

"You could have if you wanted to," Valarie corrected. "Now, you have improved your grades, you know the basics, and…" she looked at him meaningfully, "you can pull your own weight."

Amused, he paused his packing to looked down at her. "Thanks, kid."

They finished packing up in contented silence. Once everything was in order, Valarie noticed Brent was fiddling around, as if he wanted to say something but could not decide how to do it.

"Was there something else?" Valarie asked putting on

her backpack so her hands would be free to carry the lamp.

"Dr. Nee," Brent glanced around, "he's not what you think. He's a brilliant man and knows a ton about electricity and stuff."

"I don't care for him personally, but maybe he can help you keep your grades up and finish your degree." Valarie picked up the lamp.

"He's doing a kind of study." Brent shifted uncomfortably, and Valarie thought of the controlled professional this awkward, sloppy guy could become. Why was he pretending to be like this?

"Are you even listening to me?" Brent asked, bringing Valarie's wandering mind back to the present.

She gave him a half smile. "Kind of. Do you always dress like that?"

Brent pulled out the cloth of his baggy orange shirt and looked down at it before meeting her curious eyes. "What's wrong with my clothes? You got something against orange?" Brent did not give her time to respond. "You totally weren't listening to me at all. This is a big opportunity. Dr. Nee has a few questions he wants to ask you." Brent saw her frown and quickly added, "And me. He wanted to interview us both. It shouldn't take long, and he said he would give us each a hundred bucks. What do you say?"

Valarie's mind went immediately to Sedge. He had been offered money to kidnap her. Money in a hard time that seemed like it would be a quick and easy job. "No thanks, Brent. But you can if you want to."

She turned to go, but Brent fell in step beside her. "Look, kid, if he can't interview us both he won't do either of us. He wants to get answers from different viewpoints."

Valarie stopped and looked up at Brent. "He wants to get me, Brent. You are just an accessory to get him what he wants. He was really creepy in class today while you were away from the bench. I don't want anything to do with him."

Brent moved ahead to open the door for her and held it until she was through. "Come on, it is a hundred dollars. I have a future in the field of electronics, and I need this in."

"Strange how you always need stuff, Brent. You need the passing grade, need help studying, need to finish so you don't have to pay for everything on your own." Valarie looked over at him. "And you need to get this interview and money." She stopped walking and looked hard at him. "You are working for Dr. Nee, aren't you?"

A vague expression passed over Brent's face, and for a flitting second, Valarie glimpsed the professional side of Brent again. The next instant it was gone. He shoved his glasses up with a laugh. "That's crazy! Imagine me working for him with the grades I have. But I would love to," Brent told her wistfully. "Wouldn't you? He is an incredible man. All the studies he has done to make the world a better place. You should see the things he has invented. Machines to help handicaped people get around, electronics to make work sites safer and more efficient, security devices, and all kinds of things that make the world better. I want to do this interview, Valarie. Your dad can come, you can even bring the police if that makes you feel safer. But I need this."

He smiled at her raised eyebrow.

"I really want this to happen."

"I'll talk to my dad and let you know."

Brent dug in his pocket and pulled out a rumpled card. "This is the address." He dropped his backpack and crouched beside it to fish out a pen from somewhere inside. Removing the pen cap with his teeth, "It is tomorrow at ten am," he said around the pen cap as he scribbled the date and time on the back of the card. He held it out to her, and she took it hesitantly.

Recapping the pen, he tossed it into his bag before slinging his backpack back onto his shoulder. "Please come. It is really important to me."

CHAPTER 17

"You sure you want to go through with this, Valarie?" They had pulled into the parking lot of the office building indicated on the card Brent had given her. There were only three cars in the lot.

Valarie was feeling suddenly nervous. "I think so. I'm really glad you came though."

"You don't have to go in." Zach could see she was unsettled.

A movement outside the car drew their attention. Brent, wearing an ugly striped polo that clashed with his navy pants, had gotten out of an old truck and was coming toward them with a broad smile.

"Dad, I don't know why, but I think I need to do this," Valarie looked at him, and he nodded.

"It's not another hostage situation, right?"

She managed a smile, "I don't think so, but something about it seems right somehow. I don't know how to explain it."

"Alright. All you have to do is give me the signal, and I'll pull you out."

"Thank you, Dad. I don't know what I would do without you."

They got out, and Brent came forward to greet them. Zach could not help smiling at the awkward young man who stretched out his hand to him.

"I'm Brent," Brent informed Zach with a firm handshake that seemed to wilt once it had begun.

"Zach Calgen."

"And that's Valarie. Oh, but you know that," Brent stammered, shoving his glasses up.

Valarie and Zach exchanged an amused glance as Brent led the way to the entrance of the one story building. It was accented by beautifully trimmed decorative trees. Zach knew the landscaping company, and that conversation carried them in to the front desk where they were greeted by a cheery receptionist.

"I'm on my way out," she told them, picking up her purse and keys. "You are welcome to get water or anything out of that little fridge there. Dr. Nee has reserved conference room D which is the last door on this main hall. All the way back on your right. Do you think you can find it alright? I have an appointment I need to get to and was just stopping in to pick up some things on my way."

"We can find it. Thank you, Ma'am." Zach stepped aside to let her pass.

"Wonderful. I hope the interviews go well!" The door beeped, and she was gone.

They made their way down the hall. The conference rooms were marked well, and they had no trouble finding room D.

Pushing open the door, they found Dr. Nee seated at the head of the glass conference table. It was not a big room, and besides a white board mounted on the wall and a few pictures, the table and chairs were the only things in the room.

Dr. Nee rose with a smile. "I am so glad you both have come. And you, Mr. Calgen, it is good to see you again." He gestured for them to take the open seats. "For the interview, I will need to question each applicant individually. This would mean the others in the room would need to remain completely silent or wait in the lobby until the interview is over. Your answers will be recorded for research purposes. There are some extra competency tests I would like to run after the interview that are optional if you don't mind giving me a little more of your time." He saw Zach's mouth open in protest. "Mr. Calgen, I can assure you, your daughter is in no danger from me. I am a well-known professor and have colleagues in high places who can vouch for my good intents. She is a talented young lady, and I am excited to see how we can work together to allow her to reach her greatest potential."

Zach relaxed slightly.

"Of course, Valarie, you are still a little young, but I think a connection now could lead to a future collaboration that could be mutually beneficial."

Brent leaned forward, "He's saying that we could work together, and it would benefit you and his company."

"I know what he's saying, Brent. I'm 14, not three." The tension of the unknown set Valarie on edge. She saw her dad glance at her and sighed. "I'm sorry, Brent. That was rude. I will ask if I have any questions."

"Okay." Brent adjusted himself in his seat.

Dr. Nee looked amused. Turning his attention to the booklets before him, he gave one to Valarie and one to Brent. "These are just a few of the programs my company has. We are focusing now on a new program highlighting the use of electronics and electricity in assisting people."

"What kind of people?" Zach asked.

"Good question, Mr. Calgen. Right now, we are mainly focusing on how we can help and enhance the effectiveness of police and law enforcement officers. But I must admit, we have branched out some into the possibilities in the medical field. The research is fascinating. There is the possibility of giving energy in a way that enhances life and the protection of that life."

Zach looked over at Valarie who was studying the booklet with interest.

"Valarie, would you mind going first?" Dr. Nee asked politely.

Valarie looked startled and glanced over at Brent. "He wanted to do this more than me."

"Ladies first," Brent offered lamely, tugging nervously at the collar of his polo.

With a quick look at her dad for approval, Valarie nodded. "I can go first."

"Wonderful. Are you two okay with stepping out for a few minutes?"

"I would like to stay in the room," Zach informed Dr. Nee. "I'll keep quiet." His firm tone reminded Valarie of her grandpa.

"Very well." Dr. Nee pulled a little black device from the briefcase that sat on the floor by his feet. Setting the cordless recorder on the table, he pushed a button triggering a tiny blue light. "This is a recording device. It will take just a moment to set up."

Rising as if he were going to help set up the device, Brent caught himself and cleared his throat. "I think I'll get some water."

Zach frowned slightly. There was more between these two men than a brief encounter. Beneath the young man's frumpy appearance, there were subtle communications between them that Zach did not miss.

———

"That is all the questions I have for now, Valarie. Would you be open to the competency test? It is a little more in depth, however. From your answers, I can tell that you will find it well within your skill level. It will have to be a one-on-one test in order for the results to be recorded in a useful way."

Valarie looked at her dad.

"Can we have a few minutes to talk it over?" Zach asked.

Dr. Nee rose, "Of course. I will step out for a few minutes to grab you some refreshments and give you a chance to discuss." He went to the door and closed it behind him.

"What do you think?" Zach asked.

Valarie shrugged, "The questions were not hard or unusual."

"It is obvious he knows about your gift."

"Yes, but we knew that already. Dad, I'm a little nervous, but I still feel like this is what I am supposed to do. This part almost feels like I've lived it before. Like I saw it in a dream a long time ago or something." She rubbed her face. "I can't remember how it turned out."

"I don't like the fact that you would have to do it alone," Zach pointed out. "Are you okay with that?"

"What he's saying is really interesting. Dad, what if there is really a place where I can use my gifts to help people and make the world better? I appreciate that he's not trying to get me to join right away or anything. Plus, he seems happy to have you here learning about it too. It is like he is trying to see if I would be a good fit for his company, and if his company would be a good fit for me."

Zach nodded. "And you aren't getting any of those creeper vibes from all this?"

Valarie grinned. "Dad."

"I'm serious." Zach studied her face for any sign of hesitation.

Instead of responding right away, Valarie looked thoughtful. "It is strange. It seems like I should be worried or on edge about this, but I'm not. Even though Dr. Nee was super creepy watching us and stuff, after you talked to him, he totally stopped. I think I only saw him once on accident when I was running an errand with Mom. Not counting the lamp incident on the last day of class that I told you and Mom about. I don't understand him, but he does not scare me." She smiled and added, "Or give me a creeper vibe."

"I just want you to be safe, Val." He was silent for a moment, struggling through something inside. Valarie waited. Even though the programs were super interesting, she had already decided that if her dad said no, she would back out of the tests and close that door.

"I don't like the idea of leaving you alone," Zach said slowly. "But if you are okay with it, I will let you do the competency test. I'll stay in the lobby while you do it."

"I would like to do it. If you don't mind."

Zach reached out and squeezed her hand. "Lord, I pray that You would protect my Valarie. You know I love her dearly, but she belongs to you, and so I put her into Your hands. Amen."

"Amen." Valarie smiled at him. "Whatever happens, know that I love you, Dad."

"I love you too!" Zach rose and looked down at his daughter. She seemed to have grown up overnight. They talked more now, and he knew he could trust her to tell him what she really wanted. "Let's not let anything happen, if we can help it. Once was enough for me."

She nodded. "Same. If anything gets out of hand, I'll ping you with my bracelet."

Zach rose and went to the door. He was glad to see Dr. Nee conversing with Brent a little ways down the hall. They had not been listening.

Seeing him emerge, Dr. Nee walked toward him with a hopeful smile. "What have you decided?"

"She is interested in your work and would like to take the competency test." Zach informed him.

"Wonderful! It may take some time to go through all the tests. If you have errands…"

"I'll wait here," Zach interrupted.

"Of course," Dr. Nee smiled as if the news that Zach would be staying pleased him. "Make yourself comfortable in the lobby, and I will let you know when we are done." Dr. Nee assured him. "Brent, would you mind bringing some of those snacks in for Valarie?"

Brent grabbed a couple of juices from the tray on the coffee table in the lobby and strode down the hall to the conference room. He held two kinds of bottled juice. "You want grape or apple juice?" he asked Valarie.

"Grape, please."

Brent removed the cap, and Valarie rose and took the offered bottle. "Thank you."

"You want anything to eat?" Brent asked. "Dr. Nee has a bunch of snacky things in the lobby."

"No, the juice is fine." She took a sip. "Sorry you have to wait so long for your turn. Do you want to do your interview part first?"

"No, you go ahead and finish." Brent started to leave, but paused to add in a low tone, "I really appreciate you coming. Seems like a lot of lives will be changed for the good by you. You are definitely one of those energy givers Dr. Nee talked about."

She smiled gratefully and gave her Dad a quick thumbs up before going back to her seat at the table. Dr. Nee bowed slightly and followed her into the conference room. The door closed behind him leaving Zach and Brent on the outside.

CHAPTER 18

The hands of the clock were creeping around with mind numbing consistency. An hour and a half had already passed since Dr. Nee had closed the conference room door. Zach had paced, and sat, and scrolled on his phone as the minutes dragged by. Brent, despite not yet being interviewed, had left right after the test began, saying something about having time to run a quick errand.

Zach stood and moved toward the door. Was he overreacting? Was an hour and a half too long for a test? Dr. Nee had said he would have time to run errands.

Returning to his chair, Zach checked the clock again. Valarie had not pinged him. So either she was not aware of any danger, or she was not able to activate the signal. He forced himself to calm down. He was by the main entrance and would have heard the door, if they had come out.

Back on his feet, Zach paced the waiting room again as the clock hands crept forward.

Two hours. Zach moved purposefully down the hall and knocked firmly on the door. There was no response from inside. Panic welled up inside him, and he tried the handle. The door swung open revealing an empty room. The chairs were pushed in as if the room had never been used.

Zach checked the door. The lone letter D was there as it had been when they first entered. There were no doors beyond conference room D. Frantically, Zach surveyed the room. From his seat he could see the hall, but he had paced some, leaving the room out of sight for a few seconds at a time. Would Valarie allow them to take her to another location without letting him know?

Suddenly, he remembered the juice Brent had given her just before the test. His heart seemed to stop. Valarie had not left on her own.

Zach fumbled with his phone his fingers trembling as he dialed 9-1-1.

———

"She's coming to," Brent, professionally dressed and carrying himself with authority, took his seat and rolled his chair closer to his computer. His fingers flew across his keyboard. The monitors showed the room from several different angles. At his instruction, the cameras zoomed in to where Valarie was centered in each screen.

"The brain activity…wow, did you see that spike?" Brent looked up to see if Dr. Nee had witnessed the huge spike on the brain wave monitor.

Dr. Nee looked pleased. "What you just saw was a scan. In that instant she became aware of everything in the room containing electricity."

They watched in silence as Valarie took in her surroundings. Around her, on identical tables, were various electronics. Each would test a different aspect of her gift to see how developed her powers were. She rose from the chair and rubbed her forehead.

"Maybe a tad much on the drug, eh, Brent?" Dr. Nee asked without looking at him.

"I might have slipped in a little more to ensure she didn't wake up in transport," Brent confessed. "I was not sure how much she would drink."

Dr. Nee checked his watch. "She slept for three hours,

Brent, which was valuable time wasted. In future, you will remember to follow my instructions." He moved away from the control center to the observation window. On the other side of the sound proof glass, fourteen-year-old Valarie Calgen was cautiously observing the various tables from the center of the room. Dr. Nee had been keeping tabs on her from afar through various methods over the years. Now, circumstances had forced his hand to move in early. Valarie approached the first table, looking around as she went.

"How does she know how to scan the room?" Brent asked.

"She's brilliant. A lot smarter than we gave her credit for." Dr. Nee checked his phone. "I'll finish the observations. If I'm not mistaken, you have another errand to attend to."

Brent glanced at his own watch and nodded. "Being a little early won't hurt." Pushing back from the desk, Brent rose and strode from the room. He heard the click of the lock behind him as the door closed.

———

Zach watched helplessly as the investigation team poured into the building where he had last seen Valarie. Lieutenant Trice stood by Zach, offering silent support as they waited for the team to do their job. They had gone over the details of what had happened and prayed briefly together. Now, they stood watching. Both men found there was nothing else to say.

"Lieutenant, we found this in the conference room. It must have been on the table at some point. I assume the air from the vent, or the opening of the door could have blown it from the table." The man held it out, and Trice allowed Zach to take it.

Zach read the hand written note, his face contorting with anger and worry. "Why would they do this?" He shoved the note into Trice's hand and stalked away, punching his fist into his palm. They heard him muttering to himself. "I was a fool, a fool."

Lieutenant Trice smoothed the crumpled note. It read, "Valarie is safe."

———

"Hi Sedgwick, I'm here to pick you up." Brent pushed open the passenger door.

Sedge hesitated, bending to look in at the well-built, young man sitting behind the steering wheel of the black sports car. His short, light brown hair had a trendy, carefree look. Sedge estimated the driver was only few years older than himself.

"I don't know you," Sedge told him, stepping back from the open door.

"How could you forget me, Sedge? It was only, what? Five years. That's cruel, man."

"Who are you?"

Brent leaned over in his seat so that Sedge could see him from where he stood, "Look, I'm your ride. It's all squared with the police. Get in."

"Look, I appreciate the offer but…" Sedge did not finish what he was going to say.

Brent had opened his jacket slightly to reveal a handgun. "Get in."

Panic welled up inside him. Glancing over the car at the guard by the gate, Sedge saw that the older man was deep in conversation with another guard. Neither of them noticed Sedge's desperate look.

"I said, get in," Brent reached for the gun. "I won't tell you again."

Sweating, Sedge did as he was told, "Look, I just did five years for a stupid decision. Please don't make me go back."

"That will depend on you, and how useful you can be

to us."

———

"We have looked everywhere. None of her friends know where she is. The authorities have been searching for hours. Dad, I'm scared." Zach looked up to see Brook enter the room. Switching his cell phone to the other hand, he held out his free hand to her. She took it and joined him on the couch. She had been crying again. It had been 4 hours since fourteen-year-old Valarie had disappeared. The police had finished combing the office building and conference rooms for any clues. Besides the note, the only other clue was a single footprint in the dirt by the back door which confirmed their fears. Someone had left the building carrying something heavy enough to make the deep impression in the soft dirt.

Brook pulled a tissue from the fresh box on the end table and wiped her eyes. "Is that your Dad?"

Zach nodded, adjusting the phone so he could hear the retired detective more clearly.

"Any leads?" Brook asked hopefully.

A shake of his head was the dreaded answer.

"Still no response from that location device?" Reese asked in Zach's ear.

"No, it seems to have been turned off."

"Zach, I'll see what I can do. I will tap every connection I have. Don't give up. Valarie is a strong young lady, and you have given her all the self-defense training and equipment that it is legal for her to carry. I know this isn't what you want to hear, but all you can do is wait. We are doing everything we can to find her."

"Thanks Dad." Zach was glad he had not put his Dad on speaker phone.

Reese changed the subject. "Are the boys okay?"

"Yes, Brook just dropped Trent and Micah off at a friend's

house. They will watch them tonight and said they can keep them longer if we need them to."

"Good. Listen Zach, you have a cell phone, so if you want, drive around and see if you can pick up any leads. It might help." Reese understood their need to do something, even though there was nothing to be done. "You have an officer outside watching your house. Let him know you are going. He will notify Captain McKenzie if anything changes there."

"That's a good idea, Dad. We'll do that. I think it will help. Let me know if any of your connections know anything."

"Will do."

Brook took Zach's hands and bowed her head. Zach followed her example. There was nothing they could do, but they knew God was still in control. He knew where their daughter was being held.

CHAPTER 19

"Please don't make me do this," Sedge begged. "I'm not your man. I don't want to go back."

"Remember," Brent told him without sympathy, "None of the doors will open from the inside unless I make them." Brent slid out of the car, leaving the keys in the cup holder. "Stay in the car. And Sedge," Brent leaned his arms casually on the driver's side window, "feel free to start it, if you get hot."

Sedge, strapped into the passenger seat, was struggling against his seatbelt, trying to slip out to escape the car before the window was closed. Everything in the vehicle was controlled electronically. Even the seatbelt that refused to release.

Brent removed his arms, and the window started rolling up. Sedge was still desperately trying to wriggle out from under the snug lap belt.

When he reached the corner, Brent paused and pushed a button on his phone. The seatbelt unclicked on its own. Sedge dove for the doors, none of them would work. His first day out, and he was already in trouble again.

———

"Come on, Red. Can't you give me anything to go on?" Reese was leaning casually against the counter of the run-down pawnshop. "There's a kid in danger."

"Sorry, Reese, you know I'd help if I could." Red moved a stack of hubcaps from the floor and put them on the shelf behind the counter. His straight red hair was in need of a trim and hung over the tips of his ears. The suit coat he wore was dated and shiny at the elbows from use. As he turned to face the retired detective, Reese saw in his features the wear of many hard, lean years. Red's eyes flicked for an instant to the door. "You know I would help, if I could."

"You haven't heard anything?" Reese pressed, his notepad in hand. He could see the man was holding out on him.

"No, you have my word, Detective." Red squirmed for a moment under Reese's gaze. "Okay, so there's a rumor that a couple of guys are back in town." Picking up a corded drill, he turned away from the detective's trained eyes. "They aren't the type to mess with a missing teen though."

"Who are they?" Reese followed the man along the counter as he took the drill to a different shelf.

"No one of consequence. As far as I know, they are just passing through."

The door opened and a customer came in.

"You will get in touch if you hear anything?" Reese pocketed his notebook, knowing that was all the information he would get.

"Sure, sure. You will be the first to know," Red promised with an oily smile. "Now that I've done my time, I've got nothing to hide."

Thanking Red, Reese headed back out onto the street.

"Is he here?" Dr. Nee asked when Brent entered the observation room.

"Yes, traffic was smooth, and it took about an hour to get there. He's waiting in the car out back. How is she doing?"

Dr. Nee's eyes brightened. "Very well, she is working through the challenges one at a time. As expected, some are easier than others, but there have not been any that have stumped her yet. About 30 minutes more, and she should have completed all of the tests."

Brent looked impressed. Moving to the computer, he zoomed out one of the cameras to see what station she was on.

Dr. Nee's phone lit up and he glanced at the door. "Someone just entered the lab."

Turning in his chair, Brent frowned slightly at the professor's troubled look. "I thought everyone was off today. There was that announcement about routine maintenance."

The older man's eyes betrayed his concern. "There should not be anyone in the lab at this time. It is imperative that this test is completed without interruption. I need to know more fully what she is capable of. And more importantly, we need to insure she is protected. She will be an incredible asset."

"I'll check who it is." Brent rose.

"Be careful, Brent, you are invaluable to the success of this project.

Brent nodded and slipped from the observation room. He heard the latch click as he closed the door behind him.

Brent rounded the corner of the corridor and almost ran into the man standing undecided in the hall.

"Casey?" Brent blinked at him, his mind reeling. "What are you doing here?"

"I could ask you the same thing." Casey, a hard faced man with brown hair and matching eyes looked Brent over skeptically. Casey was the new head of a new wing of Dr. Nee's research department. They had worked together on a few tasks, and Casey did not take kindly to Brent's carefree attitude. Unfortunately for him, Brent was exceptional with electronics, and the young man was often directly assigned to projects by Dr. Nee. Casey knew that attempting to fire Brent would cost him his own position. This made their interactions tense at best.

"Just picking something up for Dr. Nee," Brent answered,

knowing it was a stretch of the truth.

"No one was supposed to be in the office," Casey reminded him. "Routine maintenance, remember?" His eyes searched Brent for more information.

"Ohh, was that today?" Brent shook his head, laughing at his forgetfulness. "No wonder things were so quiet." He paused, tilting his head as he looked Casey over. "If you remembered, why are you here?"

Casey glared at him, "I knew you were hiding something from me."

Displaying both his hands, Brent took a step back. "Nothing hidden on me."

"What about the observation room?" Casey asked, moving toward the door Brent had just left. "Or is that not where you came from?"

"Look, Casey…" Brent began, but Casey shoved him roughly aside.

He moved purposefully to the door and pulled out his access card. The reader flashed red.

"Locked for maintenance," Brent observed coolly. "I say we both go home."

Casey's eyes narrowed. "Open it."

"Come on, Casey. The door is locked." Brent pulled out his own card and reached over to move it in front of the reader. It flashed red.

Casey grabbed Brent by the front of his button up shirt. "I said open it."

"It is locked, Casey. Get off of me." Brent shoved him off and moved away to give himself more space. "Why are you snooping around here anyway?"

"I seem to have misplaced something I've been looking for. I think you might have it."

Brent knew by the way Casey said it, that the man knew more than he was letting on. "Well, the door is locked, so we are going to have to come back Monday for whatever it is."

"You are hiding something in the observation room." Without warning, he swung at Brent.

Brent dodged and Casey's fist connected with the wall, leaving an ugly hole in the drywall.

Crossing his arms, Brent made a show of examining the damaged wall. "And, may I ask, how are you going to explain that?"

He turned in time to see Casey's fist flying toward his stomach. Jumping out of the way, Brent heard a crunch as Casey's fist created another hole in the wall.

A second later the card reader beeped. Access granted.

Brent's face twitched with disgust. He should not have allowed himself to be distracted.

Scrambling after Casey into the observation room, Brent almost ran into him a second time. Casey stood in the center of the room, his eyes on the screen.

"Not exactly what I expected, but a step in the right direction."

Brent glanced around. Dr. Nee was no longer in the observation room. Turning his attention to the monitor, Brent watched as Valarie looked around as if she heard something. Getting her bearings, she went to the door and moved her hand along the frame to where the handle should have been. She pressed her palm against the frame. The door beeped and swung open. The computer caught one more spike in her brain waves before the sensor stopped transmitting.

Casey turned on him. "You knew she was in here, Brent. You should have warned Dr. Nee. This is the kind of power he has been looking for." His words were innocent, but Brent did not miss the anger behind them.

"He already asked her his questions when she first came in, Casey. This is not a permanent situation. This was a 6 hour surveillance."

"It is foolish to let her walk out now. That kind of power must be harnessed." He glared at Brent. "You knew about all this, didn't you?" he growled angrily.

"Casey, I know she's an incredible discovery, but she is also a minor." Brent was trying to buy her time. "If she were to partner with us, it would have to be when she is of age to make that decision. Every year she is learning how to use her powers more. If we scare her off, she will have nothing to do with our organization. On the other hand, if we treat her well now, in 4 years she may very well become our greatest asset."

"My position here was a joke, a cover-up for this." Casey indicated the observation room with a jerk of his head. "Get out of my way," he growled through clinched teeth as he moved toward Brent and the exit.

"Dr. Nee is a patient man. We have to stick to his plan," Brent protested backing away.

Casey's eyes narrowed. "Maybe it is time the plan changed."

CHAPTER 20

"Zach, I've picked up the signal from Valarie's bracelet. I'm on the far side of town, near the old water tower by the warehouse district. You can see the signal too, so I'll let you inform the police." Reese pushed open his car door and stepped out onto the deserted street. "I'm armed, and I'm going in."

"Be careful, Dad."

"I'll do what I can," Reese responded. Hanging up the phone, he shoved it into his jacket pocket and zipped the pocket closed. His pulled his handgun from its shoulder holster and put it into the right hand pocket of his jacket. Closing his hand around the butt of the gun, he moved cautiously towards the building the tracking bracelet had indicated.

———

"Valarie, this wasn't Dr. Nee's plan. Your life is in danger. Take a left."

Without questioning the overhead voice, Valarie swerved down the hall to her left. Dr. Nee, using an overhead speaker in the competency room, had warned her of danger a few seconds before. She had been in the middle of one of the harder tests, and it had taken her a minute to register the warning. Something about this male voice was familiar, but she didn't have time to try to sort it out. She ran past several closed doors, searching for an exit.

"There is a black car waiting for you out back. You need to get inside. It will take you to safety." The voice came over the intercom box up ahead. "Next right."

Valarie saw another hall and veered right. She was vaguely aware of the sound of the heavy, hall doors closing behind her.

The speaker up ahead crackled, "Open the door marked 'cargo bay' and run like mad across to the exit door. It will be on your left. I'm trying to buy you time."

She was several feet past the speaker by the time her guide finished speaking, but she caught the full message. The hall turned, and she saw an exit sign ahead. Quickening her pace, Valarie slammed into the door under the exit sign. It did not open. This was the door. It was marked with the words 'cargo bay' in capital letters. She was vaguely aware of the safety regulations posted by the door as she activated the key reader and shoved the door open. A shout echoed in the big, open room, and Valarie sprinted for the exit door to her right. Running like mad as she was instructed, Valarie saw no sign of a keycard reader by the red exit door. She hit the crash bar with both hands and the door swung open, banging into the outside wall as she darted across the open loading zone toward the street. Up ahead she saw a lone black car was parked by the curb.

———

Exhausted, Sedge climbed back into the passenger seat and reclined the back. He closed his eyes and tried to calm himself. The edges of the windows were scraped from his attack with the key and the inside of the driver's door had been partially disassembled. Sedge's efforts to get to the inner workings of the door had been stopped by the metal plate that covered them. This car was locked up tight, and nothing Sedge had tried would set him free.

"You are just locked into a car by a maniac, Sedge, nothing

major," he told himself. "You were locked up for five years. Maybe things changed a lot while you were behind bars. Maybe this is how they do probation now."

"Sedge, get back into the driver's seat." Brent's voice held a note of urgency.

Having spent years under someone else's authority, Sedge complied without argument. He did not buckle the seat belt.

A movement out the passenger window caught his eye, and Sedge saw with horror the face he had dreamt about for five years. Valarie Calgen ran to the car and opened the passenger door. Sedge dove headfirst for the door. Valarie screamed and slammed it. The door connected with Sedge's head and did not latch.

"If Sedge does not drive, the car will not go." Brent's voice came from the car speakers.

"I don't care," Sedge was holding his pounding head while still trying to climb to freedom.

Valarie stood speechless, watching him.

"Sedge, if you get out of the car, you will be a marked man. You must remain in the car."

"That's just wrong," Sedge complained. "All your scenarios end in with me going back to jail. All I want to do is go starve under a bridge in the fresh air."

"Someone is coming who will put you both in great danger. You have to leave now," Brent's voice warned. "He is no longer following Dr. Nee's orders. You must hurry."

"Brent?" Valarie asked, wondering if it were possible to suffer from a double case of shock.

"There's not time now, Valarie." The urgency in Brent's voice had increased. "Get Sedge in the car and get out of there."

Valarie could tell Sedge was struggling to think. "I think he's right, Sedge, we need to get out of here. Just sit in the driver's seat. I'll vouch for you. This wasn't your plan."

He chewed his lip weighing his options.

"There aren't any options, Sedge." Valarie glanced behind her. "Please drive it. Please take me home."

How many times had he wished he had turned back when he had kidnapped her all those years ago? Now he had the chance to do what she asked and take her home.

"Alright, get in." He righted himself behind the wheel as she slid into the passenger seat. He could tell she was battling her emotions as she raised the seat back and locked the door beside her.

"Buckle up and safe travels," Brent's voice crackled, and the radio powered off. The car surged to life. A lone figure beside the road ahead caught Valarie's attention.

"Grandpa?" Valarie craned her neck to see the person better. Was her grandpa the one Brent had been warning them about? He was hurrying towards them. Waving for them to stop.

Valarie glanced at Sedge and caught him looking her way. "What do I do?" he asked. "I'm already in this up to my neck."

The car engine revved and it pulled away from the curb on its own.

Valarie shook her head. Her Grandpa had always been the good guy, the one she could talk to and depend on. Suddenly she knew. "Pick him up."

"You sure?"

"Yes, stop the car."

Sedge pushed the breaks, but the car continued on some kind of auto drive. "I can't stop it!"

"Oh, no you don't," Valarie muttered. She put both hands on the car dash, and the car stopped with a screech of tires.

Sedge looked at her in shock. He was not the only one. Outside the car, Reese was staring at him with the same expression. Valarie pushed open the back passenger door and shouted, "Get in!"

Reese obeyed without any questions.

Once more, she placed her hand on the dash, and the car sprang to life. "Drive," she ordered.

Sedge stepped on the pedal, and the car lurched forward. In his rearview mirror he caught sight of another man who ran out onto the street a few yards behind them.

"Do you know who that is?" Valarie and Reese both strained to look.

"I don't," Valarie answered. "Grandpa?"

"He looked like Casey Heedmen." Reese looked again, but the man was too far away now to have any distinctive features. "But it can't be him."

Valarie studied his face, "Grandpa, why can't it be him?"

Reese met her eyes, "He is supposed to be dead."

———

"The tracking signal is gone." Zach tapped the screen of his phone.

"We will get to the warehouse district and go from there," Trice Higgins informed him. Over the radio he updated the other cars on the situation. Instructing them to fan out and create a perimeter around the building closest to the water tower.

"Dad's not answering," Zach worried, holding the phone to his ear for the third time.

The radio chirped and a garbled message came through. Heedmen was the only word Zach could make out. He saw Trice stiffen and felt the car accelerate.

"What is it, Trice?"

Trice did not take his eyes from the road ahead. "Pray, Zach. This thing just got a whole lot more complicated."

CHAPTER 21

The car continued to accelerate as it wove dangerously down the streets. The light was fading, but the street lights had not yet come on.

Small air bags inflated almost instantly by each of their heads, keeping them from striking the window as the car sped around the bends in the road. At Reese's suggestion, all three put on their seat belts. Sedge did so reluctantly.

"Slow down," Reese ordered.

"I can't." Sedge was holding onto the wheel and pressing the brake with both feet.

The radio crackled to life, "Get off the wheel!" Brent commanded.

Sedge's seat slid backward and his seat belt cinched in, pulling him away from the steering wheel. Sedge released it with a fearful glance at Valarie.

She sat pale and quiet in the front seat. Her arms were braced against the door and the middle console, and her feet were pressed against the floor.

"He is going to kill us all," Reese muttered angrily. "Slow down, you maniac!" he shouted at the car.

As if by magic, the car slowed slightly. Weaving in and out of traffic, they felt it slow even more. They were nearing the city limit. Once they hit the county road, it would be a long straight shot through the countryside.

Reese was muttering in the back seat.

"You okay, Grandpa?" Valarie glanced back to check. He had one foot on the middle console which allowed him to press himself into the corner between his seat and the door. In this position, the weaving of the car had very little effect on him.

"No signal on my phone," the detective responded, tapping his phone in irritation. "I got the message about Heedmen out before this crazy contraption blocked my signal."

A panel slid open on the back of the passenger seat, revealing a digital map. The numbers one through three moved along the streets of the map toward a yellow star that was moving quickly but always centered on the map.

"Alright, Pops, it's time to test your skills." Brent sounded distracted, and Valarie realized it was because he was also remotely driving their car. "You are the star. The guys who want to kill you are the numbers, got it? I'm heading out of town. Give me their positions."

Reese did not hesitate. His words were quick and precise as he relayed in real time the positions of the cars and the roads that should be taken.

The car swerved and accelerated like a terrifying video game they could not control. Despite her attempts to brace herself, Valarie's head hit the protection air bag on multiple occasions, and she was grateful it was there.

Brent's college personality had all been an act. He had been working for Dr. Nee all along. Valarie thought back over the visit she had had with Dr. Nee. He had been kind and polite, promising she would be safely returned after a few, quick tests. Was this the safe release he had in mind? Dr. Nee had honored her dad's request to stay away from Valarie until the last day of class. Why had he shown up to try to get her to use her gift to cheat? If Brent had a car like this, all of his ignorance had been an act. She had wasted hours trying to get him to grasp the simple principles of electricity when all of the time he knew a hundred times more than she did about it.

"Brent, Dr. Nee said I could go home."

"If you go home now…" he paused and the car's breaks locked, spinning it in the intersection so it could speed off down a street parallel to the one they had been on. "You will endanger your family. We are trying to protect you. Dr. Nee…." The car swerved around a bulky dump truck that was lumbering down the dimly lit street. Once they were in the clear again, Brent continued. "Casey is a dangerous man. Dr. Nee did not know Casey would strike out on his own."

"He was a fool to hire him at all," Reese informed Brent. "Keep on this road. You are three blocks ahead of them. Number 3 has peeled off to the west."

"Alright, I'll take it from here. Call the police and tell them where car 2 is located. Only that," Brent instructed. "It is a white Ford Escape. The plate number is at the bottom of the screen. Keep it on speaker phone."

Reese checked his phone again. Full signal. He dialed 911, and they listened as it rang. "Car one is gaining. He's on the parallel street east of us," Reese informed Brent who only grunted in response. The car swerved, and Valarie glanced at Sedge who looked sick. He was braced very similarly to her position, and his terrified eyes were locked on the road ahead.

"911, what is your emergency?" The dispatchers' voice came across loud and clear.

Reese informed her who was speaking and described the car and its location. "We have officers taking care of that situation," she said politely. "Thank you for calling."

"I'm making another call," Reese informed Brent. The phone was ringing before Brent could respond. The car had spun again, and they were headed back towards the city.

"Captain, this is Reese. I need you to get the officers to pick up the following cars." Reese gave the captain the information, starting with car two as instructed. Car three was next, and his signal held as he read the license plate number from the screen."

Brent's voice came over the radio. "Dark blue Nissan Sentra, dent on the front right bumper. Two occupants."

Valarie gasped, and the car narrowly missed the light pole as it swung around the corner.

"The plate for the third car is…" Reese's phone went dead. He glared at the console. "Heedmen is in car one, isn't he?"

The car swerved for what seemed like the 50th time. Valarie and Sedge were both trembling with the effort of keeping themselves from flying into the sides of the car as it randomly changed directions.

"Why won't you let me turn him in?" Reese demanded.

Brent did not respond. The car sped down a dead end toward a brick wall. A fearful whimper escaped Valarie's lips. She felt her seatbelt cinch a little tighter. The wall loomed closer. She suddenly knew that Brent was not going to stop.

"Don't you dare," Brent's voice was pinched with concentration. "You stop it now, and it is all over."

Valarie couldn't think. Paralyzing dread surged through her.

"Trust me, kid," Brent pleaded, rapidly closing the distance between the wall and the car.

"Car one is one block over, turning this way," Reese informed them. They could hear the fear in the older man's voice.

Valarie closed her eyes and instinctively put up her arms to shield her face from the glass. The impact never came. The car screeched to a stop inside a large empty room with a polished cement floor. It pulled around casually to face the entrance. Stunned, they watched in silence as a metal wall descended to seal the hidden entrance.

They all sat dazed, unable to move.

Valarie's door was opened from the outside and she looked up to see Brent, the professional version, holding the door open for her. He wiped the sweat from his face, and she saw that his dark dress shirt was also damp with perspiration.

"We made it," he said with a weak smile. "Thanks for not interfering. Skid marks outside cancel out the secrecy of the hidden entrance."

Reese pushed open his door and stepped out unsteadily. "Why wouldn't you let me report Casey Heedmen?" he repeated.

Brent's chin rose slightly in response to the detective's accusing tone. "He is not in car one, Mr. Calgen. I know this is a lot to take in, but honestly you were never part of the escape plan. I assume Valarie activated her tracking bracelet when she escaped, and that is how you found her. My job is to protect her at all cost." Brent patted Reese on the shoulder. "But your navigation updates were very helpful. I'll admit, that one was a bit of a nail biter."

Valarie still sat in the car, her eyes closed. Tears streaked her tense face.

Noticing for the first time the scrapes that cut through the tint covering the passenger window, Brent leaned in to run his finger over them. "Dude, what did you do to my car?" He released the passenger door and went around to the driver's side.

An exclamation of despair accompanied his discovery of the lacerated door panel. "Why?" he asked incredulously. "You totally vandalized my car!" Brent put both hands into his short hair, holding his head as if it would explode. "Seriously, Man. You shredded the inside of the door. And the window too! Do you have any idea how much this will cost me?"

Sedge glared at him, making no move to get out.

CHAPTER 22

Stalking away from the car, Brent checked the four monitors that filled one of the tall workbenches against the far wall. Every once in a while he would glance at his car and shake his head as if unable to grasp the damage. "Brent Starclish. Begin lockdown procedures," Brent spoke to the computer in a clear, steady voice. The screens changed as the device responded to his command.

"Car number one has passed the entrance and is continuing on up the street," Reese informed him.

Brent's fingers moved rapidly over the screen of his phone. The cover slid over the screen in the car that Reese had been looking at, blocking it from view.

Reese went to the passenger side of the car and helped Valarie out. She was shaky from the prolonged rush of adrenaline.

"There are snacks there on the other side of that counter. Drinks are in the fridge. You are welcome to whatever you want." Brent shot an irritated look at Sedge. "Though it is more than some of you deserve."

"You kidnapped me," Sedge pointed out. "I don't feel bad about it at all."

"And you kidnapped her," Brent shot back pointing at Valarie. "But she didn't rip your interior to shreds." Brent realized Sedge had not moved from the car. Turning his back on him, Brent said dully, "You know you can get out whenever you want, right? Your job is done."

"What kind of lame joke is this?" Sedge demanded, scrambling out of the car. "You forced me to join your…" Sedge gestured to the strange surroundings trying to come up with an appropriate insult. "Your little video game reality, where every scenario you don't get to run ends with me going back to jail. What am I supposed to tell the police when they pick me up for my involvement with a psycho maniac?"

"I'll take care of that." Brent looked slightly amused, but did not condescend to returning insults.

"You needed me as a decoy in case something went wrong." Sedge was usually an easygoing person. When he had been locked up, he had allowed himself to dream about being free again, but nothing had happened as planned in the hour since his release. The terrifying drive caused Sedge's emotions to surge, and he made no effort to control his anger. "You are totally throwing me under the bus when you are the one who hired me to kidnap her in the first place!"

Reese and Valarie looked at Brent in shock.

"Oh no, looks like you forgot to tell them that tiny detail." Sedge's smile was almost cruel. "Deal with that, Hot Shot. I kept my mouth closed during the interrogations so people wouldn't find out about her superpower. I took the heat and did the time because I felt bad about hurting her. All that time, you were the one hunting her down. It looks like you might need to tell them who you really are." He stalked across the room to the corner where a rectangle rug and five padded chairs created a sitting area in the corner of the spacious room. To his left was Brent's computer set up. The screens glowed with security footage and what seemed like random images and code, but Sedge made no effort to decipher any of it. He passed the snack bar and fridge on his right without hesitating. Turning to face them once more, Sedge slumped into one of the chairs where he could keep an eye on the others. The opposite side of the room was open and empty with the exception of a single empty workbench against the far wall.

"Is that true? Did you hire him to kidnap Valarie?" Reese's firm tone held a threat.

Brent stepped back, trying to keep an eye on both men. "You two settle down. We can talk it all out later. I'm trying to keep you from getting killed."

"I asked you a question," Reese pressed, moving toward him. Even though he was in is upper sixties, Reese was still fit enough to be imposing.

Glancing over at the monitors once more, Brent turned to face his accuser. "Yes, I hired him. She was not in any danger. He had express instructions not to hurt her in any way. The gun wasn't even loaded. It was supposed to be a couple of quick questions and everyone would go home safely. Valarie could have avoided it all, but she wouldn't talk to the plant in the park that we hired."

Valarie made a face. "Why would I talk to a plant?"

Reese was still moving toward the younger man with steady, calculated movements. "You mean you hired someone to pry information out of my granddaughter?"

"Not pry, Mr. Calgen. We got a nice, safe mom with a child to ask a few questions and pass on a little information in a non-intrusive way. Only the kid here would not give her the time of day."

Valarie remembered the overly-friendly blond lady who always seemed to show up at the park when she and Jessie were there to play. They had become very good at avoiding her.

"So why didn't you ask me at school?" Valarie could see no trace of the sloppy classmate version of Brent. "I was there twice a week for months."

"Okay, so rub it in." Brent was losing his cool. "I took a whole semester of the most boring class in the history of education so you could learn the basics. Not to mention the other classes I had to sit through to get myself a school reputation and make the whole thing believable. You could have had a private class and worked on some actual electronics that mattered. But no, you had to waste hours getting the information in a classroom of lame students."

"You hired a desperate man to kidnap her, and then, four years later, posed as a student in her class?" Reese was not happy.

"She needed to know the basics in order to strengthen her gift," Brent responded without actually answering the question.

"They will book you on so many charges that it will make your head spin," Reese informed him coolly.

Putting some space between himself and the detective, Brent walked to the food bar he had pointed out earlier, his movements purposefully calm.

Reese could tell that despite his careless air, the young man was keenly aware of the location and movements of all three of his guests.

Retrieving four bottled waters from the fridge, Brent set them on the counter. He checked the computer screens from where he was, and glanced over to where Sedge sat brooding to his right. "All that could have been avoided if you had talked to that nice lady in the park."

"It is not Valarie's fault, Brent, it is yours. You paid Sedgwick to kidnap her," Reese observed, shifting the blame back to Brent. "Kidnapping is illegal. You should have spent time behind bars with Sedgwick."

Approaching warily, Brent handed Reese and Valarie each a bottle of water. "The kidnapping, as you call it, was supposed to be a ten minute job. Only, Zappy here had to delay everything and get Sedge thrown in the slammer before he could get her across town."

Valarie looked over at Sedge who sat with his head resting against the back of the chair. She could tell he was rapidly losing hope.

"Since we are all blaming each other, why don't you consider the guy who got power happy and started waving around the empty gun?" Brent asked. "It was his choice to take the job. No one forced him to do it."

"You knew I was in a tight spot and needed money," Sedge countered, coming to life again. "The hotshot here offered me a thousand dollars to transport you across town. Only I didn't get a penny, and I lost five years of my life."

Brent reached for his wallet and pulled out a thick stack of $100 bills. Closing the gap between them, Brent shoved the money into Sedge's hand. "If it was up to me, you wouldn't get a penny after what you did to my car." He looked over at Valarie. "The $100 Dr. Nee promised you for doing the test will be mailed to your house. Is everyone happy now?"

"What did you do, rob a bank?" Sedge sat up to examine the stack of cash in his hand. "There's a lot more than a thousand here."

"Don't cry to me about it." Brent told him over his shoulder as he returned to the snack bar. "Everything else is my fault, but that is not." Brent grabbed the two remaining waters from the counter and tossed one to Sedge. He crossed the room toward the four monitors, taking a swig of the water as he walked.

Reese broke the silence. "That money does not clean up all the loose ends."

Brent froze with his back to them. He knew enough about law enforcement to know that the steady, firm tone Reese had used was almost always accompanied by a weapon of some kind. Brent's hands moved out and away from his core. "We are trying to do the same thing, Mr. Calgen," Brent's voice was steady. "We both want to protect Valarie." He turned slowly as he spoke, his eyes immediately locating the handgun Reese was pointing at him. Licking his lips nervously, Brent's eyes darted to the sitting area. Sedge still sat where he had been. Reese saw the relief in the young man's eyes.

"We have different opinions about the meaning of safe, Mr. Brent," Reese informed him. "Where is Casey Heedmen now?"

Brent's eyes moved from the weapon to the face of the retired detective. "I would have to look at the screen."

"Look at it then. But keep your hands where I can see them."

Brent glanced at Valarie who stood watching from a safe distance away. She could power the car and the door in the blink of an eye, and they both knew it.

Rotating slowly once more, Brent enlarged the map with a single key stroke. His eyes scanned the small lines of text that were auto generating in real time. He turned to face Reese and the gun. "He's off the grid. I don't know where he is."

CHAPTER 23

"Honey, we know she is safe. That was the last message we got from her." He read the text to her again. "Safe with g-pa."

"But that was an hour ago, Zach. That is not how she texts."

"Brook, if she had only a blink of signal, she would not waste her time on grammar."

Brook buried her face in her hands. "What is wrong with the police? Why can't they find her?"

"I'm sorry, Mrs. Calgen. We are doing all we can." An officer had entered the waiting room in time to overhear her questions. "We found both of the cars called in by Detective Calgen, and there was no sign of Valarie in either one. The Nissan that was supposed to have two occupants only had one man inside when we caught up to him. There is no evidence that the second occupant was your daughter. The other car was abandoned. We are doing our best to locate the driver. The text you received from her, Mr. Calgen, came at the same time as the tip from your dad. Knowing him, she is in a safe place."

Brook was trembling. "Just because they are both missing does not mean they are safe."

"We are questioning the suspect now and will let you know as soon as we have anything solid to go on," the officer promised. He crouched in front of Brook and looked her in the eye. "Mrs. Calgen, most of our officers have kids of their own. I promise you we are doing everything we can to bring her home safely."

Nodding, Brook wiped her tear stained face with both hands. "I know. I'm sorry. I just want my baby back."

"That is what we want too. I know you don't feel like eating, but I am going to send out some sandwiches for you both."

She nodded again, and Zach thanked the officer as he rose.

"I'll let you know when we hear from them again," he promised.

———

"Mr. Calgen, please put the gun away." Brent had been standing for almost half an hour under Reese's watchful eye. "I told you before, I could not keep track of Casey and get you all away safely at the same time."

"Grandpa, he's right. At least let him sit down."

Valarie rose from the chair she had been curled up in and went to where Reese sat. He had moved a chair for himself where he could keep Brent in his sights. "You've had him standing there forever."

Brent waited silently.

"Turn around," Reese instructed after thinking it over. "Stay out of the way," he told Valarie as he approached Brent from behind. "Put your hands behind you."

"Come on, detective, can't you give me a chance?" Brent felt the cold metal of a handcuff wrap around his wrist. The empty water bottle he still held was removed from his hand.

"You have no authority to cuff me," Brent suddenly protested.

A rookie would have pressed his gun into Brent's back to show his authority, but Reese Calgen was no rookie. He stepped back, making it impossible for Brent to gauge where the weapon was. "Nice try. Go sit by the computer bench."

Valarie saw Brent's shoulders sag as he moved to obey.

A thick metal bar attached the two wheeled legs of the

desk to give it support. Once the chain that attached the handcuffs was around that bar, even standing would be impossible unless one of the cuffs were unlocked.

"Grandpa, what if he is telling the truth? What if Brent is trying to help us? He helped me get out of the building and told me about the getaway car. I would not have made it out if he had not told me where to go."

"Wrap that cuff around the leg and click it tight around your other hand." Reese ignored Valarie's petition.

Brent lowered himself to the ground beside the desk. Leaning his back against the side of the desk, he pulled the second cuff behind the desk's leg and over the metal brace bar. He hesitated, but one look at Reese told him there was no point in pleading for mercy. The click of the metal cuff echoed through the large room.

Valarie was aware of a slight surge of electricity and instantly the computer screens went dark. She turned. The light in the key pad by the door had also gone out. She looked at her phone. There had been a very weak signal when they arrived. Not enough to send anything, but enough to allow her to hope it would increase. Now, there was nothing.

"You have the gift, too," Valarie breathed softly in surprise.

Brent made no indication that he had heard her. He leaned his head wearily against the wall and closed his eyes.

Reese motioned to Valarie. "Valarie, turn on those computers and see what you can find. But stay away from him."

Valarie went around her grandpa's chair to approach the far side of the desk. When she pushed the space bar, she was not surprised to see the lock screen pop up.

"I can't unlock it, Grandpa. I don't have the password."

———

"Jessie, right?" the man leaned his elbow out the driver's window and pulled the car to the curb beside her.

Crossing her arms, Jessie pushed the SOS button on the tracker on her belt with her concealed right hand. "Who wants to know?"

He laughed cheerily, not seeming to mind her rudeness. His rusty brown hair was cut short and the waviness of it reminded Jessie of the lake water when the breeze blew across it. Wisps of gray wove through his hair. Jessie noticed this because, though there was something hard about his face, he did not seem to be much older than Valarie's dad.

"You have every right to be careful, young lady," the man said with a smile. "I won't hold it against you. I came to ask if there was any news about your friend. I have seen you two all over town together for years, and when people heard she was missing, I wanted to help, if I could. My wife would have come, but she's down with a cold and didn't want to make things worse."

Jessie thanked him politely for his interest and informed him that they had no further leads on Valarie's location.

"Why do you think someone would kidnap her again?" His eyes were probing behind his friendly expression. "This is the second time, and right after that man got out of jail again. No one seems to know where he is either."

Again, Jessie thanked him politely for his interest and informed him that they had no further leads on Valarie's location. The police had been very clear that she was not to give any information to anyone outside of the investigation.

A look of annoyance crept onto his face. "There is nothing special about Valarie Calgen?" he asked, trying to seem friendly.

"She is my best friend, Sir. There are a thousand things that make her special to me." Jessie saw a police car turn onto Park Street a few blocks away. Jessie stepped away from the car, signaling the end of their conversation. He pulled in his arm, and the car moved away from the curb. By then, the police car lights were on and flashing.

Jessie's lips moved silently as she repeated the license plate number to herself. She stood watching as the stranger's car sped away, noting the direction he turned and the street he had turned onto. Once he was out of sight, Jessie pulled out her phone. Remembering details was a game she and Valarie had played for fun many times over the years. But today, it was not a game.

CHAPTER 24

"Brent?"

His eyes opened instantly, and he glanced around the room before meeting her curious gaze. Reese was dozing in his chair, the gun resting on his thigh. Sedge had moved to the floor and was sleeping on his side on the rug, his face creased by an uncomfortable frown.

Valarie sat cross-legged a few feet from Brent's long, stretched out legs.

He looked at her with tired eyes and waited.

"Why did you bring Sedge here?" she asked quietly.

Brent glanced again at the dozing detective. "He took a lot of heat for a job he botched. But it was a job I asked him to do. I guess I felt responsible to help him get his feet under him again."

"You work for Dr. Nee, don't you?"

A simple "yes" was his answer.

Valarie had expected it to be harder to get out of him. "And Casey Heed-whoever?"

"Heedmen. In a way, I worked for him." Brent paused, as if trying to concentrate. "But he was under Dr. Nee as well. He is a good man, Valarie." Seeing her confusion, he added quickly, "Dr. Nee is a good man." Shifting, Brent tried to find a better position for his arms. He glanced at Reese whose breathing was still steady.

Valarie glanced at her grandpa. "You have at least half an

hour if you are quiet," she told Brent with an amused twinkle in her eyes. "You might need it to answer all my questions, so I'll try to make it fast."

Shifting uncomfortably, Brent waited.

"You turned off all the electric controlling access to the outside."

Brent chose not to respond to her soft observation.

"And the computer monitors." Valarie sat forward. "I saw you do it."

"The computer tower is right here on the floor behind me," Brent pointed out.

Reese shifted in his high backed seat and sighed.

"Valarie, your grandpa is waking up." His tone was urgent. "Please promise me that you will not leave this building until you hear Dr. Nee's voice."

Valarie blinked at him in surprise. She had expected a plea to be freed from the handcuffs. This request caught her off guard.

"I can't make a promise like that," Valarie answered seriously.

"Valarie, listen to me. You don't know Casey. He is a shrewd man and very dangerous."

"Yet he worked for Dr. Nee," Valarie pointed out not letting him finish.

"It is complicated, kid." Brent leaned his head against the wall once more. "Ever heard the saying, 'Keep your friends close and your enemies closer'? Dr. Nee wanted Casey close enough to stop him."

"But he got away," Valarie pointed out.

Brent's eyes moved to her face. "So did you."

Valarie understood and did not respond. Brent and Dr. Nee had gone out of their way to keep her from getting hurt. After passing the class, she had agreed to the interview with Dr. Nee with her dad's reluctant permission. Neither had realized how long it would be, or that her tracking bracelet would be disabled during the observation time. She knew her parents would be sick with worry. Besides the one text she had slipped out during her Grandpa's permitted call in the car, she had not been able to contact them.

"Would you let me call my parents?"

She saw his resolve waver, noticing for the first time how tired he looked.

"I'm sorry, kid. I can't."

"They will be worried." She pulled her knees up to her chest and rested her chin on top of them.

"I know. It can't be helped. Casey is too close." A bead of sweat ran down the side of his face, and he wiped it on the shoulder of his shirt. "You will have to hide if they get in." Brent shifted again on the hard cement floor. "There is a trap door to the safe room in the snack/kitchen area. It is under the fourth tile from the far counter. Just scan it and find it. Take some water and something to eat down there with you. It might be a little crowded, but you will all fit. It's not too bad down there, it even has a bathroom." Brent's attempt at a cheerful tone was not convincing.

She frowned at him, and his expression became serious.

"Signals can be tracked. We can't chance it. Look, Valarie, you have no reason to trust me, but I'm asking you not to leave this building." Laying his head against the wall, Brent sighed and closed his eyes.

Valarie sat watching him for a minute, his brow was creased slightly like it did in class when he was focusing on something. He was generating power of some kind. She thought of the night she had powered the hospital generator, and suddenly she understood. She knew how to give power, to activate things. Brent was blocking power, essentially disabling access to the computers, the building, and whatever else he was controlling. At the same time, he was powering some kind of invisible shield that made the building un-detectable. To do both at once would take a huge amount of energy. Yet Brent had somehow managed to carry on a conversation with her at the same time.

With a new sense of respect, Valarie moved away from him.

————

"Anything?" Zach and Brook asked hopefully as the officer passed through the room.

He shook his head, "Not since the last update. The information from Jessie helped us locate the car Casey had been driving. It was located south of town in the old business district. Rest assured that the area is now crawling with cops."

"He could have stolen another car and be miles away," Brook worried.

"Yes, but we believe your daughter has something to do with why he is here. All of the leads and sightings that have been called in, have been within a 20 mile radius of the city. They have also come from all over the city and its outskirts, meaning Casey somehow knows she has not left town, but he has not yet located her."

Glancing at each other, Zach and Brook allowed themselves to hope.

"I am on my way out there and will radio in if there are any updates."

They nodded and thanked the officer.

"Why did I let her do that test?" Zach asked banging his fist slowly against his knee. "I should have seen this coming."

"She wanted to do it, Zach. We both know that. Her classmate spoke to her at the college, and she had already decided she wanted to participate in Dr. Nee's interview."

"It was supposed to be a few questions and an observation period. Now it has been over 10 hours. What a fool I was!"

Brook put her arm around his and held him tightly. "Zach, your dad is with her."

"We don't know that." Zach pulled away and stood. "She could be anywhere right now, Brook. We have no idea where either of them are. Dad could be dead for all we know!"

Brooks face paled. Zach knew she was thinking the thought that had just shot through his mind. For all they knew, Valarie could also be dead.

———

"Mr. Calgen?" Brent's voice had lost its jaunty air of authority.

Sedge rolled over and looked at Brent through the gap between chairs. He got up, rubbed his eyes, and stretched before sauntering over to where Reese sat snoring lightly.

"What do you want?" Sedge asked.

"Can you wake him? I can't feel my arms. If I could stand up for a minute." Brent could see Sedge was not in favor of the idea.

"Why did you bring me here?"

Brent's eyes were red, and he squinted as if it were hard for him to focus. "To save your life, Sedge. You were a hot target." Brent made an effort to shift his position. Wincing, he gave up and slumped against the wall again. "Look, I need your help. Can you wake him? Or get the key?"

Sedge could see it was not an act. Brent was drenched in sweat and sagged against the wall like a wilted plant. "I'll get you some water." He headed toward the snack area, touching Reese on the shoulder as he passed. The older man roused with a start. His grip on the butt of the gun tightened, and Brent ducked his head instinctively.

The detective had not lost his skill. His finger rested safely on the side of the gun instead of on the trigger. He looked across at Brent without compassion.

"You win, Mr. Calgen," Brent told him. "I can't feel my arms. Or my backside for that matter. My back is killing me. Would you let me stand up, just for a few minutes?"

Sedge passed Reese with a bottle of water and a protein bar he had found in the cabinet.

Rising, Valarie walked slowly towards her grandpa. Taking a deep breath, she stepped between the gun and Brent. "Grandpa, you need to let him go."

Reese shook his head, not able to understand the sudden shift in loyalties. "Get out of the way, Valarie."

"No, Grandpa. He saved our lives, and you need to let him go. You made your point. He's not going to try anything." She moved closer to him and held out her hand. "Give me the key."

"I don't trust him, Valarie. You don't know about this kind of man."

"No, I don't. But I don't believe he is the kind of man you think he is." Her hand remained out, ready to take the key. "We are going to have to stick together if we want to get out of this."

Reese let his breath out in an irritated blast. She was standing too close for him to rise without colliding with her. "Get out of the way, Valarie."

She stood firm, her expression serious. Behind her, Sedge was holding the water so Brent could get a drink from it. Valarie felt the electricity fluctuate slightly and glanced back at them.

Brent moved his head away from the water, his attention on the door. "You have to get to the safe room, now!" His tone was urgent. "Valarie, listen, there is a green light inside, make it red and keep it that way." Valarie grabbed Reese by the wrist and pulled him along toward the trap door. She located the invisible panel and activated it. Six of the grey and white tiles that made up the snack bar floor began to rise.

"Get in, Grandpa, don't touch anything!" She crossed the room to Brent and picked up the cold water bottle Sedge had left beside him. "I'm sorry."

"Get to the safe room, now," he ordered.

Sedge did not stop to ask questions.

Brent's face was pained with effort. The keypad light flickered on for an instant and went out again. "Now, Valarie, go now!"

Valarie ran.

CHAPTER 25

"Zach, Brook, we have a new lead," Trice announced as he burst into the room. "Someone just spotted Casey and two other men prowling around that old car sales building in the old business district. It has been boarded up for years, but seems like that is where all of the action is leading. No, no." He stopped them as they stood. "You are going to have to give us space to do our job."

"We have to go to her. We have to help her," Brook pleaded.

"I gave you the update because I told you I would." Trice looked them both in the eyes. "Now you are going to have to do your part and stay put. I wanted to tell you myself because several callers reported that all the street lights around that building blinked the SOS pattern twice before returning to their normal functions."

Brook gripped Zach's hand. "Oh, Zach, she's okay!"

"But what can we do?" Zach asked Trice desperately.

Trice gave him a hopeful smile. "Pray hard, Zach. A lot of good people are putting their lives in danger, and we are going to need some supernatural intervention."

———

"Brent Starclish," Casey laughed cruelly. "Looks like you got on the wrong end of the deal this time."

Brent met his mocking gaze. "I underestimated the sway of a 45 caliber, if that is what you mean. Now that you are here, you can let me out." He nodded at the two men flanking Casey. "Greg, Destin, you always were the front line type. Isn't this a happy reunion of co-workers? You got your wire cutters handy, Greg?"

"You never did know when to keep your big mouth shut," Casey growled. "Where is she?"

"The electric kid?" Brent asked bitterly. "She ran off with the old detective after he equipped me with these sturdy handcuffs." Brent's jaunty act seemed hollow even to himself, but Casey did not seem to notice. "Come on, guys, do an old pal a favor. I've been sitting here for hours."

They only smirked at him.

"And you expect me to believe that you let them go?" Casey asked doubtfully.

"It wasn't like I had much choice," Brent pointed out. "Besides, he had a nice sized handgun on his side."

Looking him over skeptically, Casey grunted with distain. Apparently believing and dismissing Brent's story at the same time. "Search the place."

Greg and Destin spread out to search the big room. A few minutes later they returned. "There is no sign of anyone else." Greg informed Casey.

Destin interjected, "There are a few water bottles and chairs like this one out of place, but the condensation on the bottles has already neutralized in temperature."

"Meaning?" Brent asked.

"Meaning that if they left, it would have been more than 30 minutes ago."

"The only noticeable electric source in this room is right here with the computer Brent is by," Destin confirmed. "I unplugged the fridge."

Casey pulled a handgun from his concealed holster.

Destin slipped under the desk and checked the back of the computer. "Nothing."

"Come on, Casey," Brent pleaded. "They already trashed my car. At least let me keep the computer."

Toying with the firearm, Casey cocked his head towards the car.

Greg walked around to the driver's door and pulled it open. He smirked over the top of the car at Brent. "This is going to cost you a pretty penny to repair."

Brent only glared at him.

"The interior is trashed," he confirmed.

"This doesn't seem to be your day, Brent." Casey cocked the gun and pointed it at the computer tower. "We are looking for someone who can produce energy, and your little computer is getting in the way of the signal."

"You think she's hiding behind the computer?" It was Brent's turn to smirk. "She's not that little. If you are so keen on shooting something, why not hit this chain and let me out?"

"You helped them get away."

"They took my car. I wasn't even in it," Brent corrected.

Dustin closed the trunk of Brent's car. "He's got a point. He wasn't in the car. I saw him leave the office after you two went after his car. He was on his phone and didn't see me."

"Thank you, stalker D," Brent muttered.

"What were you doing on your phone?" Casey's gun was still trained on the computer behind Brent.

"Casey, think about it. You deliberately crossed Dr. Nee, endangered the girl, and my car drove away without me. What do you think I was doing on my phone?"

"For a sweaty, helpless mess, you sure are belligerent," Casey observed coolly.

Brent glared at him. "How about giving me a hand instead of rubbing it in?"

"I don't think so." Casey sneered. "You are out of my way here, and that is how I plan to keep it." He turned to his men. "Anything?"

"No, the car is clean. No other electronic signals are detectable besides the computer."

Uncocking his gun, Casey shoved it back into its holster. "Alright, let's move. Enjoy your stay Brent. It might be a long one."

———

"Hello?" Zach asked, touching the screen he turned his phone on speaker so everyone could hear.

"This is Dr. Nee." The Asian professor's voice filled the silent office.

Around him, several officers leaned forward. One held a notepad while another monitored the recording on the computer before him. A third watched a map on another screen as the computer honed in on the caller's location.

"Doctor, where is Valarie?" Brook demanded.

"I am very sorry I cannot tell you at this time, Mrs. Calgen." Dr. Nee's voice came through the phone. "There are many unexpected things we are dealing with to the best of our ability. Your daughter is with my best man, and her safety is our number one priority."

"We want you to bring her back," Zach informed him.

The officer with the notepad set the pad on his knee and put his hands palm up in a questioning gesture.

"Where is she?" Zach demanded.

"I know you must be very concerned, Mr. Calgen. Please know I share your feelings for her welfare," Dr. Nee responded. "Her location must remain unknown for her own safety." He paused and then added, "There are others besides the police who can track and intercept calls. Do not waste your time. I am not with her now. Officers, Casey Heedmen is armed and dangerous. Greg Tirod and Dustin Childs are also in town. Both are working for Heedmen. This is their last known location."

A pop up window appeared on the locating computer. "Look at this," the officer hissed.

Another window appeared and disappeared from the screen in a flash that was almost imperceptible. The map they were observing zoomed out, moved, and zoomed in again on another part of town.

"Did he just hack the police station computer system?" Zach asked softly.

The officers did not respond. One moved away to transmit the new location to the officers patrolling the area for any sign of Valarie.

"Once you have stopped Casey, Valarie Calgen will no longer be in danger," Dr. Nee informed them.

"How do you know she is safe?" Brook interjected, trying not to cry.

"I trust my men to do their job." The phone beeped, and he was gone.

CHAPTER 26

"You have to free him, Sedge," Valarie whispered. The room they were in was a six by ten foot rectangle lined on both sides with parallel, wooden benches. The dim LED light in the center of the ceiling cast eerie shadows on the walls.

"We aren't exactly friends." Sedge looked over at Reese who was brooding on the bench that lined the other wall just a few feet from them. "Any of us," he added.

"It looks like we need to set that aside and work together if any of us want to get out." Valarie focused once more on the little device beside the trap door that led to the big room above. The light had flickered green for an instant.

"Is that hard?" Sedge asked, gesturing with his chin at the little box.

"It takes some concentration," Valarie responded. "Don't you see, Sedge? That's why Brent needs help. He has been…" She turned the light red again but made no effort to go on.

"He has been what?" Sedge asked skeptically.

"Locked up a long time." They both knew that is not what she had started to say. "Look, I'll go if you don't." Valarie stood up, and Reese looked over at her.

"What are you doing?" he asked.

"I'm getting Brent," Valarie informed him. "If you two don't have a heart, I will do it myself."

Reese turned to Sedge, "Get up there, Sedge."

"Me? What am I, the scapegoat?" He would have said

more, but Reese's hard look silenced him.

"Stop the whining. I'm going with you." Reese stood and moved toward him, and the door.

"That's a real comfort," Sedge muttered. With a sullen face, he turned to the wooden stairs. "How do we know it is clear? If we pop up like gophers they might just knock us off."

Both men looked at Valarie.

"I don't know. Could you crack the door and listen?"

"Is it worth jeopardizing us all?" Reese asked.

"Grandpa, Brent is a person too. We don't understand everything that is going on, but I do believe he is trying to help us."

"You can't always tell…"

"I can," Valarie interrupted, and he fell silent. "I'm sorry to be rude, Grandpa. But we do not have much time. If he turns out to be a bad egg, I'll help you take him out."

Biting his lip to smother an amused grin, Sedge started up the wooden ladder.

Reese shook his head. "This goes against every instinct I have."

Valarie hugged him quickly. "All you have to do is get Brent and get back without being spotted."

"Right." Reese slid past her to stand by Sedge. "You follow my lead, you hear? This means stop." He held up his palm. "And this," Reese beckoned, "means come."

"I'm not stupid," Sedge muttered.

One of Reese's eyebrows went up. "You kidnapped a child for money. As far as I'm concerned, your sanity will always be in question. Once we open that door, there will be no more talking. Casey Heedmen knows what he is doing. If Brent is still up there, and still alive, it means Casey probably left a listening device. Brent is the bait to draw us out."

Sedge didn't bother to respond. He moved up the stairs and slid the well-oiled latch out of the way. Looking back at

Valarie, he crossed his fingers.

She folded her hands as if she were praying and nodded at him.

Pushing the door up slightly, Sedge waited. There was no sound from the room above them.

Reese gave him a nod, and Sedge moved upward, opening the door as he went. Again, he paused, there was no sound. Even the refrigerator beside them was silent.

Sedge slipped out, crouching on the tile floor as he waited for Reese to emerge.

Reese made his way out of the trap door, crouching stiffly beside Sedge. He pointed toward the counter, and Sedge rose slowly to peer over it. His eyes scanned the big open room. Ducking, he shook his head and gave the detective a thumbs up.

Reese put a hand up, signaling Sedge to remain where he was. Slowly, gun in hand, the detective moved from behind the shelter of the counter. He paused to listen. Standing, he walked softly across the room to where Brent was slumped against the wall. Pulling the key out of his pocket, Reese released the cuffs, holding them carefully to keep the chains from clinking together. Brent's arms hung limp, and he made no effort to rise.

Reese scanned the room again before beckoning Sedge to join him. Moving Brent's arms, Reese re-cuffed his wrists in front of him, keeping his hand around the curved metal to muffle the click. Sedge knelt beside the detective, shooting him a questioning look. Neither spoke. Sedge shook Brent, but there was no response. Moving the tall man away from the desk, Sedge slid his arms beneath Brent's arms from the back, gripping his own wrist in front of Brent's chest. Feeling Brent's chest rise and fall, Sedge shot a hopeful look at Reese who wrapped his arms around Brent's legs just above his knees.

Reese nodded once, and they heaved him up from the ground. The tension was palatable as they once again crossed the open space to the snack bar. The trap door was still open. Reese descended first so that Sedge could take the stairs frontwards. Even so, the younger man stumbled under the weight. If Valarie had not grabbed his arm, he would have taken the last few steps at a higher speed than intended. Valarie scrambled up and secured the trap door. Turning the light on the little box red again, she stepped from the stairs to the bench. The stack of water bottles wobbled, and two fell onto Brent who took up the floor between the benches. He groaned.

"That's one way to wake him up," Sedge observed, swiping a granola bar from beside the drinks and moving around Brent to sit on the far side of the little room.

"Where did all that come from?" Reese asked.

"Sedge handed it down while he waited for your signal," Valarie answered cheerily. She tossed him a water and a pack of gummy worms. "Enjoy."

Brent groaned again, his face tight with pain.

Valarie slid around and held up his head to give him water. Instead, she succeeded in pouring water down his neck. He gasped and coughed. His eyes opened, and they could tell he instantly knew where he was. The first thing he looked at was the little box. The light was green. His eyes met Valarie's.

———

Greg slipped into the hotel room and closed the door softly behind him. Greg was unknown in this area. Having evaded the police pick-up during the car chase, he had been the one to book them a room in the cheap hotel on the edge of town. It had been simple to distract the clerk while Casey and Destin slipped in through the back door. Edgar, the fourth member of their little band, had figured out that they were being tracked and had managed to drop Casey off without detection minutes before the cops surrounded his car. Because Detective Calgen had called the car in, and because of Edgar's record, Edgar would be out for the duration of this run.

"Anything?" Casey lay on one of the full sized beds with his hands laced behind his head.

Looking at Greg expectantly, Destin closed the book he had found in the dresser drawer.

Greg shook his head. "Nothing. Brent is gone. The hand-cuffs are gone too.

"What about the car?" Destin asked.

Greg got himself a drink and emptied his glass before responding. "It was there. It hasn't moved or been run."

"Too bad we can't use that to make our break." Destin turned to see what Casey thought of the idea. Getting even with Brent was something that was rising on his "to do" list.

"It is one of those electrical cars. With that girl on the loose, I wouldn't bank on anything electronic around here." Rising, Casey moved to the imitation leather chair on the edge of the tiny sitting area. "There was no evidence of how he got out?"

"Nothing. The bar he was chained to is scratched up a little but that is the only evidence that he was there at all. The only reading on the bug we left on Brent's computer was the quiet scuffling sounds I went to check out. They must have known about the bug, because it did not even pick up the sound of the doors opening. I looked around, and there was not a footprint to go on. Tracking a detective is bad business if you ask me."

"I was too soft to leave him there," Casey reflected angrily. "Somehow, in the last two hours, Brent and Dr. Nee have managed to round up and hide the three people I came here to deal with. I want their location."

"The area is swarming with police, Casey. Apparently a navy veteran reported a street light blinking SOS."

Smiling, Casey leaned back in his chair. "That was sloppy. Even for Dr. Nee."

CHAPTER 27

Brent was awake now, pacing stiffly up and down the narrow aisle. His lively smile had been replaced by a tired, worn look. At Valarie's insistence, the cuffs had been removed. Brent stretched his arms now and then, trying to reduce the stiffness. They had spoken very little since he had awakened. They had all eaten and now sat watching Brent pace.

The light on the box was red again, and Valarie kept it that way.

"How long do we wait?" Sedge asked for them all.

Rubbing his face with both hands, Brent sighed and turned to them. "Until we hear from Dr. Nee."

Reese was the next to speak up. "He knows where we are?"

"He knows where we should be," Brent answered vaguely. As if the thought had just occurred to him, he felt his pocket for his phone. His eyes went to the trap door above.

"Not a chance," Reese spoke in answer to his obvious thoughts.

"If I had it…" He looked around at the tired little band and fell silent. "It won't work anyway."

"If you did have it, what would you pay?" Sedge asked mysteriously.

"Sorry to disappoint you, Sedge, but you have all the cash I had." He sat on the steps, rubbing his face again.

"It won't work because of this box?" Valarie asked.

"My phone? No, by keeping the light red, you are blocking

signal and sound. There is a larger one out there, but it takes a lot more energy to operate."

"How would you know?" Sedge looked thoughtful as if trying to formulate the hint of an idea.

Brent gave him a half smile. "Because I built it."

———

"Destin, how long have you been with me?"

Looking up, Destin studied Casey for a moment before answering. "Six…seven years. Why?"

Casey looked thoughtful. He leaned back casually, causing the fake leather of the hotel chair to creak in protest. "Greg, when did the cops break our streak?"

"About six years ago, I guess," Greg answered casually from where he lay watching TV from the hotel bed. Aware of Casey's thoughtful, brooding mood, Greg had kept the volume low in order to stay alert to the boss's movements.

"We had a good thing going," Casey observed. "If Sedgwick Harrison had not shown up, we would have walked away with millions."

"If it hadn't been for that rigged kidnapping stunt, we would have taken care of him already," Greg reminded him.

He was rewarded by an angry glare from Casey. "That's what I mean. How did Sedgwick know we were at the bank? How did the police show up so fast?" Casey leaned forward, turning his attention to Destin. "How was it that almost a year later, just before we bumped him off, Sedgwick gets picked up by the police and hidden away for five years? None of his pleas were accepted, and he didn't get a cut in time for good behavior. That's not the way the system works. Which means someone was working the system. I wait for five years for him to get out, and then someone swoops in and snatches him out of our hands at the gate of the prison."

"Where are you going with all this, Casey?" Destin asked

distractedly, his attention going back to his book. Though he was not looking at Casey directly, he was keenly aware that he was being watched.

"It seems to me that the line of coincidences is too long to be called coincidental any longer. Sedgwick Harrison disrupted the electronics that night. That one incident cost me over a million dollars."

Glancing up, Destin turned the page. "It almost cost you your life, Casey." His eyes returned to the book in his hand, but Destin was no longer reading the words.

"Shot down like a dog," Casey remembered bitterly. "A whole year of my life wasted. What are you reading?" Casey demanded when Destin did not respond.

"Some kind of history book." Destin checked the cover. "Holy Bible, by Gideon," Destin read. "It doesn't really matter. I read to wind down. You know that."

"Put it away," Casey ordered.

After a moment's hesitation, Destin set the book aside on the short couch which was to be his bed for the night. Though he obeyed, Casey could see Destin was riled. Glaring across the room at nothing in particular, Destin waited.

"I say we pull a heist tonight," Casey announced.

Both men were instantly alert.

"Are you sure, Casey? You aren't just restless with all that's going on?" Greg sat up and swung his legs over the side of the bed. He watched Casey intently.

"The whole police force is held up tonight with the search of the electric girl, Greg. What better time to slip in and slip out?"

Greg weighed the pros and cons silently. After a few minutes he met Casey's eyes. "The job seems a little sudden, but you are the boss. I am in if you think it will work."

Casey shifted to look at Destin, "And you?" he saw the uncomfortable look in Destin's face.

"I agree with Greg. There's not much time to prepare."

"Do you have a problem with that?" Casey asked, his eyes locked on Destin's face. "Or is there someone you need to talk to first?"

"Who exactly are you afraid I am talking to?" Destin challenged. "At some point, you have to face reality. The last time you tried to rob this bank was six years ago, and you nearly got killed," Destin pointed out. "The bank security would have changed since then. Plus, the equipment is still stashed away at Red's and will have to be retrieved before we can do anything."

"Do you have a problem with that?" Casey's look was deadly.

Shrugging, Destin rose and adjusted his shoulder holster. "Fits me better than hunting down a kid. I'm in."

Shrugging into his jacket, Destin went to the door.

Casey narrowed his eyes. "Where are you going?"

Frowning darkly, Destin turned to face him, obviously struggling to contain his anger. "Do I need to get a pass now to leave?" He stood tall, challenging the reclining leader. "Are you doubting my loyalty, Casey? If that is what this is about, why don't you say so?"

Casey took his time responding, allowing Destin's anger to increase.

"Don't you think it is strange, Greg, that Destin joined my band just before the heat from the cops?"

Destin's chin went up. "Reese Calgen laid you out for your funeral with that shot six years ago. If I wanted to cross you, I would have done it then. I risked my own life to help Edgar get you out." Not waiting for permission, Destin pulled open the door and left the room.

———

Reese checked his watch and reached down to shake

Brent's shoulder. Brent had asked them to let him sleep thirty minutes in order to recharge. After Reese agreed to wake him, Brent had stretched out on his back on one of the wooden benches. He had fallen asleep almost instantly.

Now, he opened his eyes and quickly assessed the room. Everyone was there and the light by the door glowed red.

Reese stepped back to take his seat between Valarie and Sedge, who sat as far away from them as possible.

Closing his eyes again, Brent sighed.

For a moment, they thought he had gone back to sleep.

Sitting up in one smooth motion, he looked at them with a half-smile. "Ready to conquer the world?" The transformation was incredible. It was as if he had literally recharged while he slept.

They exchanged glances to see if what they were seeing had really happened.

Brent stood with a groan. Stretching his back and arms, he walked the length of the room and back a few times. "You all should see yourselves. Just sitting there staring like you have never seen someone so good-looking in your life."

Valarie grinned at him, her eyes laughing. Reese and Sedge made no response to his attempt at humor.

"When can we get out?" Sedge asked. "I had more room in jail than we do here."

"I know, and I am sorry." Brent was serious again. "Casey will make his move soon. Once he does, the police will pick him up, and we are free to go."

"How do you know he will make his move?" Reese asked. "He has been off the streets for six years."

Brent shook his head. "Not really. He's been sticking to small jobs, ones that keep him under the police radar, waiting for Sedge here to get out."

Frowning, Sedge looked at the others for an explanation.

Valarie shrugged. She knew nothing beyond what they

had just heard.

Brent made another tiny lap. He placed both his palms on the ceiling of the cement room and stretched again. "I never thanked you for risking your necks to bring me down here. You definitely went against my instructions, but I'm grateful you did." He rubbed his wrists and added, "And thanks for removing the cuffs."

"I removed this too." Reese held up Brent's hand gun.

Brent patted his right hip and smiled. "Thank you. That thing makes me nervous. I'm always afraid I'll shoot a hole right in my own leg. I'll leave the shooting up to you. Only, if it is not too much trouble, I'd rather not get shot. And don't take out either of them." He gestured at Valarie and Sedge. "I'm kind of responsible to keep them alive."

"I think we let him sleep too long," Sedge told Valarie. She nodded in agreement.

————

"Ah, I was hoping to see you before you left town."

Startled, Destin automatically stepped away from Dr. Nee. He tripped on an uneven square of the sidewalk where the tree roots had pushed their way through the cement, and fell hard.

Dr. Nee held out a hand to help him up. "Are you okay? I did not mean to startle you."

Scrambling to his feet, Destin knew immediately that something was wrong with his left wrist. "I was clumsy, that's all."

"Where is Casey Heedmen tonight?" Dr. Nee asked.

"He's..." Destin retrieved the computer bag he had lost in his fall, wincing as he swung the strap over his shoulder. "He's moved on to other things."

Dr. Nee's keen eyes grew concerned. "You are hurt?"

"I'll be fine. I didn't see you come up." Moving away,

Destin hoped Dr. Nee would take the hint and let him go.

"I expected Casey to go, but was sorry to see you quitting when this level of research is so close to completion." Dr. Nee went on casually.

"It was not a good fit for me anymore." Destin was backing further away. When he turned to go, Dr. Nee followed, walking beside Destin as one would do with a friend.

An idea came to Destin, and he stopped in the thick shadows of one of the oak trees that lined the sidewalk. The street lights were spaced far enough to leave a space of darkness between the rings of light. "You mean you would take me back?" he asked trying to make his voice sound hopeful.

"Is there a reason you should not come back?" Dr. Nee inquired.

Destin shrugged, "I thought it was over now that the electric girl has disappeared." They walked a little ways before Destin broached the question. "Do you know where she is? I heard on the news that her grandpa, Detective Calgen, was missing too."

Laughing, Dr. Nee stopped to face him. "It seems we both have information the other one wants. Perhaps we can find a middle ground."

Something about the way he said it made Destin uncomfortable. "Maybe another time, Dr., I have a lot on my mind right now."

"When?" Dr. Nee asked pointedly.

Destin glanced around before meeting the professor's eyes. "Tonight."

CHAPTER 28

"I wish I had my phone," Brent bemoaned to himself glancing at the red light on the wall. He walked over to it and gripped it with one hand. A moment later, the box buzzed and opened. Brent flipped the switch inside and shut the box again.

"It had a switch?" Valarie demanded, slouching wearily against the wall. "Why didn't you flip it before you slept?"

"I could have died and you would have been stuck," Brent explained.

"But you could still die," Valarie pointed out.

With a shrug, Brent helped himself to one of the remaining water bottles. "It doesn't seem as likely now." He chugged the water, emptying half of the bottle.

"You don't have your phone, so how are we going to know when Casey makes his move?" Reese asked what they were all wondering.

"Yeah, it sure would be nice to know right away instead of having to wait until Dr. Nee can come release us." He looked at Sedge who was not meeting his eye. "That could be hours after the action, depending on how it goes down."

Valarie looked over at Sedge. "Sedge, do you have his phone?"

"Why would I have it?" Sedge asked, too quickly.

Valarie looked questioningly at her grandpa, and he nodded discreetly.

"We all know you have it, Sedge. Give it to Brent or we will be down here forever."

"Fine." Sedge pulled out the phone and tossed it at Brent who caught it easily. "It doesn't work anyway."

Brent glanced at the little box and sat down to check his phone. The screen lit up and his fingers moved over the screen.

"How did you?" Sedge caught himself and muttered, "I couldn't even get it to light up."

"It's not polite to use other people's phones without permission," Brent laughed. "It is a little touchy about who uses it." He glanced knowingly at Valarie.

She was the only one who knew how Brent's phone worked only for him. Either it did not have a battery or its battery source was not strong enough to power the phone on its own. Brent's touch was what powered the phone. Somehow, it was programed to react to power just like a normal phone would react to the screen being shut off. She remembered the hours she had spent explaining the basics of electricity to this genius and blushed at her own stupidity.

Brent glanced over at her, saw her red face, and seemed to know what she was thinking. "Don't sweat it, kid."

Reese glanced at Valarie. He shot a disapproving look at Brent, but the young man had already returned his attention to the phone screen.

"But if you can't get a signal in or out with that light lit by the door, what good will your phone do?" Valarie asked.

Brent's eyes flicked toward the box. The light was green.

Sliding her phone out of her pocket, Valarie unlocked the screen. Her fingers moved quickly across the letters. She hit send and braved a look at Brent. He was watching her, amused. He dropped his gaze to her phone before meeting her eyes again.

She looked at her screen. The message had failed to send. The light by the door was red again. "Seriously!" Valarie slumped back, defeated.

"Don't take it so hard. I've got some good news. Casey is planning a move. Dr. Nee guessed he would try something when he could not get his hands on the three of you," Brent announced cheerily.

"Why does he want the three of us?" Sedge asked. "He's a detective, she's a kid, and I'm a worthless deadbeat with a record. They," he gestured at the Calgens, "knew each other, but I was a total stranger until you roped me into this mess." He reached over and snatched a granola bar from their dwindling supply. "It doesn't make sense, and I'm tired of being involved."

"Maybe it is time for me to tell you all a story," Brent observed casually.

———

"Dr. Nee received a message from his man. It said 'all safe.'" Chief McKenzie himself had come to let the Calgens know. He was a big-boned man with a thick, old fashioned mustache.

"That's all?" Zach asked softly. Brook's head rested on his shoulder, her face troubled even in sleep. They had been allowed to hold their vigil in the officer's break room where there were a few couches and a round table with chairs. This offered more privacy and allowed them to be both protected and easily located.

Chief McKenzie's face softened. "Don't lose hope, Zach. Valarie is safe. We all had our doubts. Even you. But it is good to know she is okay."

Relaxing a little, Zach nodded. Brook felt the movement and lifted her head.

"Valarie is safe," the chief told her before she could ask.

Brook sat up eagerly. "Where is she?"

"We don't know yet, Brook," Zach told her gently. "But

they know she is safe."

"What about your dad?" She looked from Zach to Chief McKenzie.

"It said, 'all safe' I can only assume that means all," McKenzie answered for Zach.

———

"When their crime ring moved here, that is where your grandpa got involved." Brent stretched out his long legs and crossed them at the ankle as he turned his attention to Reese Calgen.

"The local bank had gotten in the new shipment from a bigger bank," Reese said, taking up the narrative. "We are a moderately small town, but our bank was a holding point for cash that is moved on to the bigger cities up the interstate. That night, all the new money was added to the old and locked away in the bank vault."

Brent made no attempt to take back the narration.

"We had gotten word that Casey's gang had been seen heading this way. Chief McKenzie called me up and asked me to see what I could find out. He was afraid his officers would botch it by jumping in too soon. I started poking around and was able to confirm that the rumors were true."

"So it all came down to a showdown at the bank on a Saturday night," Brent said, speeding up the story. Reese took the hint.

"We had a stake out and had set a perimeter around the bank. Only this bank robbery was not the kind we were familiar with. He was not after the physical cash in this bank. Casey had rigged up electronics to transfer the money from some high level accounts to his own dummy account where he could move it again without detection. As the night drew on, I realized we were missing something big. I crossed the street and waited. I'll admit, I prayed." He glanced at Valarie.

"Your dad is rubbing off on me, I suppose."

She smiled.

"Something down the street caught my attention, and I followed the hunch. A moment later, I saw a figure slip by and disappear into that deep entrance of the old federal building. I knew right away that this was the building an expert like Heedmen would choose. He was as slippery as an eel, and one of the smartest criminals I've ever encountered. I radioed it in, crossed the street and…"

"Anything you want to add, Sedge?" Brent cut in. He and Valarie had both seen the change in Sedge. Surprised, Reese turned to look at the pale young man.

Sedge's eyes darted to the trap door, looking for a way to escape. "I wasn't involved. I hadn't even heard of Casey Heedmen."

"Tell us what you remember." There was an unusual hint of compassion in Reese's tone.

Licking his lips nervously, Sedge complied. "I had just been informed by my landlord that I had 24 hours to clear out of my apartment." Sedge looked as if he feared they were teaming up to pin the whole crime on him. "I needed some place to collect my thoughts. I didn't know they were robbing the bank."

"But you heard about it later," Brent pointed out.

"Yeah, everyone did. It was all people were talking about. I didn't have a TV, but someone told me that a detective killed the guy who was the brains of the operation." Realization dawned in his expression, and he looked over at Reese. "You were the one who shot him."

CHAPTER 29

"Casey knows you talked to Dr. Nee. He wants to see you." Greg informed Destin from the shadows as he approached the hotel's back entrance.

"Are you his little stool pigeon now, Greg?" Keeping his head down to keep his face hidden from the hotel cameras, Destin pushed past him and opened the door.

Noting the computer bag Destin carried, Greg followed him inside.

"Here he is, Boss," Greg said from behind Destin as they entered their room.

Casey was cleaning his gun.

"Oh, this is classic." Destin was careful to use his right hand to lower the computer to the couch. "I feel like I just walked into a scene from a detective novel."

"Maybe you have read too many of those kinds of novels," Casey suggested ominously.

"One thing I've learned is that once the boss stops trusting his men, the whole set up falls flat on its face." He pulled a small, dark box from the bag. "I assumed we would need this for the job tonight so I took the liberty of picking it up from Red. I ran into Dr. Nee on the way back. Almost literally. I was polite, dodged his questions, and came back a round-about way, once I was sure I was not being followed. Anything you don't like about that?" Destin waited, meeting Casey's glare without fear.

Casey's expression softened slightly. "Greg may be a little on edge tonight. I guess it checks out. Sit down. What did Dr. Nee want?"

"Wanted to know where you were. I told him you had moved on to other things." Destin was unpacking the contents of the bag onto the couch. The compact transmitters would make it possible to do what they needed to do from outside the bank. Though their size also limited their range, their method was similar to the electronic signals sent by the girl. Only she didn't believe in robbing banks. At least, not yet.

Casey looked amused. "Always truthful, eh, Destin."

———

"So Casey saw Sedge go into the entrance of the federal building just before his equipment started shutting down?" Valarie looked at Brent for confirmation. "And he must have thought that Sedge had something to do with it. That he could control electricity like..."

Brent's eyebrows rose slightly.

"Like I can." Valarie finished without looking his way.

"Exactly," Brent agreed gratefully. "Sedge had nothing to do with what went down there. He was, and is, completely innocent."

"But that is not how Casey saw it." Sedge was thoughtful.

"And what happened next?" Brent prompted.

Reese was also thinking hard about this new information in connection with all they had gone through. "I radioed in my position and that I was going in." He stopped and looked at Brent. "If he thought Sedge was the one blocking the signal, then that explains why he came into the lobby alone."

Brent nodded.

"But what happened, Grandpa?" Valarie asked, sitting forward on the bench.

"I went in, armed and ready. You never know what to

expect, and I knew it could be my last walk."

"Don't you ever get scared about what will happen if you get killed?" Valarie blurted the question as if she could not hold it back. Something caught her eye, and she saw the light by the door was green. Brent set down his phone and it turned red again.

Valarie shot Brent a withering look.

Reese had missed the whole exchange. His answer was hesitant, "You know, sometimes I do wonder about what will happen."

"But you know how to be sure where you will go when you die," Valarie pointed out. "How can you stand not knowing?"

"I think we are getting a little off track," Brent observed.

"Jesus paid everything, Grandpa. He covered your sin that separates you from God. All you have to do is believe it is true." Valarie moved to sit by him.

"I know," Reese said quietly.

"Aaaand back to the important story we are reviewing," Brent prompted.

Valarie stood and faced Brent. "Do you want my grandpa to die and be separated from God forever in hell?" she challenged.

Brent's eyes widened in surprise, "Wow, I guess that would have to be a 'no.'" He turned his still wide eyes on Reese. "If you are going to deal with that right now, Sedge and I can wait."

"We aren't doing anything," Reese responded, embarrassed. "Where was I?"

"You were going across the street to where I was," Sedge reminded him. "I saw him coming with that gun and made a run for it up the street. I thought you were the guy who got shot when I heard about it later."

"Thankfully not," Reese glanced at Valarie who was miffed at his dismissal of eternity.

She drifted over to take her seat again on the bench across from them.

"I barely had time to step inside before I saw Heedmen storming towards me with his gun drawn." Reese went on, "I guess I was a little more focused than he was because his bullet hit the glass door behind me when I plugged him in the chest. I can't say which happened first. He dropped immediately. I heard his men coming and backed out while I had time. The doors of the federal building are bullet proof so I pulled out quick to put something between the gunmen and myself. The police came swarming a few minutes later. When they went in, the gang and Heedmen were all gone. They found a trail of blood, but it ended at the curb. It didn't take much brains to figure out that someone had loaded him into their getaway car." He looked at Brent. "That bullet should have killed him. Everyone said so. The security cameras caught the shot, and the medical experts said it killed him on impact."

Brent shrugged. "Even the experts are wrong sometimes."

———

"But at the same place?" Chief McKenzie asked incredulously. "He must be crazy. Are you sure that is what he was telling you?"

"Yes." Dr. Nee glanced at his phone. "The three are safe. Brent is telling them why they are being protected."

"Who are the three?" This was the first time since the disappearance of Valarie Calgen that Chief McKenzie had gotten any actual facts. Everything else had been second hand or hearsay.

"Valarie Calgen, Reese Calgen, and Sedgwick Harrison."

"Sedgwick?" Chief McKenzie's brow furrowed. "Isn't that her kidnapper from five years ago?"

Dr. Nee nodded. "His life crossed Casey Heedmen's path

the day Casey was shot. Casey does not forget. If it had not been for his desire to kill all three, he could have easily killed the detective and his granddaughter. He has been in town several weeks.

"And you did not let us know?" Chief McKenzie demanded. "You were a fool to wait so long, Dr. Nee. We could have picked him up without all this extra danger and expense."

"Perhaps so, but there are other factors I had to consider." Once again, he glanced at his phone. "The day he was shot, there is nothing that can be proved, besides the fact that they were in the federal building after hours. There was no equipment found, the money was not stolen, he could have shot at Detective Reese out of self-defense." Dr. Nee paused to let the facts sink in. "Casey Heedmen works clean, and though we all know he is behind the string of robberies and killings across the country, he leaves no evidence behind."

"Where are they now?"

"They are all at the little ground level hotel next to the Breakfast Burrito. When I intercepted Destin, he had the equipment with him. The plan is to make the move tonight."

"They are down a man. I have Edgar locked up." The chief was pleased to have something to show for the long day's work.

"That is fortunate," Dr. Nee agreed. "I have given you much today, and I will ask only one thing in return. You must not kill Destin Childs." He stood and fished a picture from the inside pocket of his suitcoat. "Carrying this was a risk I should not have taken." He laid the picture on the chief's desk.

Chief McKenzie picked it up. The man in the photo was not looking directly at the camera when the picture was taken. Instead, his dark serious eyes seemed to be focused on something just to the right. His square jaw and dark hair made him hard to forget. "I assume this is Destin Childs,"

Chief McKenzie looked up, and Dr. Nee nodded once.

"Without him we would not have Casey at all. But we do not have much time. I have confirmed that the three are still safe, but you must move quickly. Take Casey and Greg, but protect Destin. He is a good man and has given much to bring closure to this case."

"I will do what I can," Chief McKenzie responded. He pushed a button on his desk intercom, and the door opened a moment later. "Notify the men that we will be moving out. We have a location for Heedmen."

The officer looked pleased and turned to obey.

"And Sergeant."

The man paused in the door way. "See that they circulate this picture. This man is to be taken alive if possible."

"But Casey must not know this," Dr. Nee inserted.

"Right. Got it." The Sergeant crossed the room to retrieve the picture. He left, pulling the door closed behind him.

"Alright, Dr. Nee. Sit back down and tell me everything I need to know."

CHAPTER 30

"After that, we assume that Destin, Edgar, and the others took Casey somewhere to be treated. We lost track of him for almost a year."

"Who is we?" Reese asked.

"That's not pertinent to the story," Brent answered with a mysterious air. "When we found out he was headed here, we moved in to high alert. The three of you were instant targets, and we knew Casey would do everything he could to take his revenge. Men like Casey Heedmen are seldom crossed because they are very good at tying off the loose ends."

"What does that mean?" Valarie asked.

"Killing them. Casey kills people who hurt him or cross him," Sedge answered, before the others could. "Or the ones he thinks have crossed him," he added soberly. The facts were falling together, and he understood now Brent's claim that he was trying to protect them.

"Oh." Valarie sat back. She knew Brent was the one who had interrupted the bank transfer Casey was doing. Casey should be gunning for Brent, not Sedge. Brent should have been the one to sit in jail to be protected for five long years. Was there no other way to keep Sedge out of the criminal's reach?

"You okay?" Brent asked, and Valarie realized she had been frowning at him, lost in her own thoughts.

"Yeah." She looked away, afraid she would blurt out the

unfair truth. As long as no one knew, Brent was free to come and go as he pleased. It was right that he too was trapped in this box-like room with them. Without him, none of them would be there.

"Is there something you need to have explained?" Brent's expression was concerned.

Shrugging, Valarie pulled her feet up onto the bench. Wrapping her arms around her legs, she rested her chin on her knees. Reese would have described her action as a textbook example of a self-protecting movement. She was dealing with something she did not want the others to know.

"I'm sorry I trashed your car." Sedge's statement caught them all off guard. "I didn't understand."

"That might take some time to forgive." It was hard to tell if Brent was serious. After a pause, Brent added, "I'm sorry you had to go through so much because of me."

Sedge frowned slightly, but Brent did not explain.

———

The swat team was geared up and ready. Their last assignment had produced no leads. Now, they had the target location and were ready to move. It had been a long day for them all, and they were ready for closure.

"The suspects have exited the hotel."

A few men adjusted their ear pieces. Their unit was divided into four positions around the Federal building. Their mission was to keep the suspects from escaping the perimeter, once they were inside.

———

"So what about the kidnapping?" Reese asked.

"We knew Casey was in the area again and gunning for Sedgwick here. So we created a win/win situation. Hiring him to transport Valarie got him off the street, brought him to us, and allowed Dr. Nee to talk to her."

Reese cleared his throat, "Why did he want to talk to her?"

"We needed to know what kind of kid she was. Was she able to stand up for what is right, or was she swayed by the influence of others?"

"Weren't you pretty young yourself?" Valarie asked.

Brent grinned, "Old enough to make a difference."

She frowned slightly, that was something Dr. Nee had said to her during the interview.

"Besides," Brent leaned in with mock confidentiality, "I'm older than you think I am."

"What about the other win?" Sedge asked. "You said you had a win/win situation."

"If you got picked up, you were still off the street and protected."

"So it was a win/win only for you," Valarie observed.

"Depends on how you look at it." Brent was not willing to agree. "Only you hid your gift well and were an incredibly creative and stubborn nine-year-old. You did that trick with the lights and brought the police all in one sweep." Brent looked Valarie in the eye. "You saved his life."

"What do you mean?" She wanted to hear more about it.

"You were already in transit when we discovered Casey had a man staked out along the route with a powerful riffle. He would have killed Sedge and probably you too. Because of your antics, he never made it to the ambush point."

Sedge looked at her gratefully as if seeing her for the first time. In his eyes, he had been an unwanted failure. The more he heard, the more that viewpoint shifted. All those years, there were people interested in his wellbeing who were willing to go out of their way to protect him. His view of life was shifting rapidly.

———

"What's with your arm?"

Destin realized he had been favoring his sore wrist as he drove toward the federal building. "I tripped and caught myself to keep from breaking the equipment earlier. It won't get in the way."

Casey eyed him skeptically.

"If you don't trust me, how can I trust you?" Pulling up his left sleeve, Destin kept his eyes on the road.

Casey saw the purple bruising around Destin's wrist, and said nothing.

"Greg will meet us there with the equipment," Destin recounted. "I'll drop you off and join you once I stash the car."

"The plans have changed."

Destin glanced over at him, but Casey was looking at the road ahead.

"Okay." Destin did his best to keep the fear out of his voice. "You are the boss. Where to?"

"There is an empty lot up ahead. Pull in there and back the car up into the brush," Casey instructed. He could see Destin was nervous.

Maneuvering the car into the lot, Destin shifted into reverse. "All the way in?"

"All the way," Casey confirmed.

With a nod, Destin slid the car part way into the brush. Sweat trickled down his back. "Do you want to get out before I pull the rest of the way in?"

Considering this, Casey pushed open his door and got out. He stood watching as Dustin slid the car backwards into the brush. Branches screeched against the sides of the car.

When Destin looked up through the windshield, Casey was in front of the car holding his handgun.

———

"Where did Casey go when I was arrested?" Sedge asked.

"He skipped town. The fact that Reese was the one who shot him was not public until some loose mouthed friend made a comment about it at his retirement party a few years ago. Apparently, word got back to Casey, and he started to make plans. We have had a mole," he glanced at Valarie, "an informer on the inside who is trusted by the bad guys."

"I know what a mole is." Valarie did not bother to lift her head from her knees. She was tired and wanted desperately to go home.

"Right, so our mole let us know he was coming back to town. Casey is rarely impulsive, and his patience makes him a terror in the crime world. He knew when you got out, Sedge, and he knew if he killed just two of you, his chances of getting the last one would go down."

"So he planned to sweep through town and knock all three of us off once Sedgewick was out?" Reese had been sitting with his head bowed and eyes closed.

Brent laughed. "I thought you were asleep."

"Just resting my eyes," Reese responded.

"No wonder you are a great detective! Yes, that was the plan. And that is why I picked you up at the gate, Sedge. Casey was being extra cautious this time. Bringing in only three of his closest men."

Sedge stood and reached into his pocket. Pulling out the thick fold of money he had been given, Sedge held it out to Brent. "Use it to fix your car."

"Dr. Nee was right about you." Brent's eyes shone with gratitude. "But no, Sedge, the money is yours."

"But I was only promised one thousand," Sedge protested. "You can have the rest."

"Dr. Nee had someone invest it for you when they put you away. That wad is what it turned into over the five years. Don't worry about my car. It was hard to swallow at first, but one car for three lives is an impressive exchange. Besides,

I might have done the same if someone had trapped me in an incredibly cool car like that one." His eyes sparked with fun. Brent saw Sedge was struggling with his emotions and gently pushed the handful of money back toward its owner. "For real, man, it was what the car was made for."

Sedge looked at the money in his hand. More money than he had ever owned. Tears welled up in his eyes. He retreated to his seat, turning away from the others to hide them.

"But how did you get Grandpa to be there to be picked up?" Valarie asked.

"Did you activate your tracking bracelet when you escaped?" Brent knew the answer.

She looked thoughtful. "I don't remember."

"No, you didn't. I left Sedge outside," Brent considered adding 'tearing up my car,' but the young man seemed to be dealing with a lot, so Brent omitted the extra jab. "I activated your bracelet knowing the sleeping detective here would be on the way in an instant."

"Resting my eyes," Reese repeated, raising his head. Valarie smiled at him.

"But she made the car stop," Sedge pointed out. His eyes were red, but he was regaining his composure. "How did you know she would stop the car?"

CHAPTER 31

Greg tapped his fingers nervously on the briefcase. The transmitters were set up. Everything was ready for the connection, but Casey and Destin had not shown up. They did not have much time. It occurred to him that he could make the transfer and get the money.

Glancing around, as if afraid someone would have overheard his thought, Greg touched a key on the laptop. The lock screen appeared. Greg had been with Casey long enough to know what would happen to anyone who crossed him. Casey Heedmen was a hard man who did not forgive. Greg stepped away from the laptop. Looking over at the desktop computer on the other section of the L desk, Greg confirmed the replay loop of security footage was working. Replaying the previously recorded scenes made it possible for them to slip in undetected and do what they needed to do. The number in the corner counted down ominously to when the system would return to live recording. Greg steadied himself. If he were caught now, the whole racket would be pinned on him.

Checking his watch, he glanced around the spacious office. Their window of opportunity was closing fast.

———

Destin sat frozen in the car, his eyes locked on the gun in Casey's hand. His fearful, questioning gaze moved up to Casey's hard eyes. The brush blocked the car door. For an instant, he wondered absently if the owner would mind the extra scrapes along the sides. It did not matter now. His blood on the seat would probably be more disturbing.

He suddenly realized that Casey was grinning.

Frowning, Destin tried to make sense of the odd behavior. He saw Casey gesture for him to come. Pushing his door open against the protesting branches, Destin heard Casey's cold laugh.

"Pull the car up."

Destin obeyed slowly as Casey stepped out of the way.

Casey glanced around impatiently.

Once the car was out of the brush, Casey got in and shut his door. Resting his gun on his thigh, he looked over at Destin.

"Just had to be sure. This is going to be a big job you know. Drive on."

"Sure of what?" Destin tried to keep the tremble he felt out of his voice. Pushing the gas, he steered the car back onto the street.

Casey shrugged.

Adrenaline was kicking in. "You did all that as a joke?" Destin's voice wavered with rage. "To test my loyalty?"

"It pays to be sure," Casey answered casually.

"Sure of what?" Destin's volume was increasing. "Sure I was yellow? Sure you could kill me in a side alley if it tickled your fancy?"

Casey's look was cold and hard. "Sure you wouldn't cross me. Because now you know what it would feel like if you did."

————

"I've been protecting Valarie for several months now. I've gotten to know her a little. She was nice enough to help an awkward nobody with his studies. So, I gambled a little on her stopping the car," Brent responded. "If I am honest, I was ready to settle for best out of three with Casey running out right behind you."

"Why not just shoot Casey?" Sedge asked, shoving the money back into his pocket.

"It is illegal to shoot someone for running after a car," Brent informed him. "If he had pulled a gun, we could have justified it, like Detective Calgen was able to do. We had men ready to protect you, Mr. Calgen, if it is any comfort. You would have had to take a different car though." Brent looked at each of them with a satisfied smile. "And you know the rest. After a harrowing drive and some handcuff drama, we all made it here. Now that you are safe, the wheels upstairs can start turning."

"You are driving the car again?" Valarie asked raising her head. "Do you do it with your phone or that computer up there?"

Brent looked confused for a moment and then laughed. "I meant the wheels of justice or something noble like that. Not the car." He laughed again at her disappointed expression. "I do use my phone. It's like a wildly intense video game that you can't afford to lose."

———

Destin pulled up to the curb and looked over at Casey. In the last few minutes of the drive, Destin had wondered if the crime leader was cracking up. Even this robbery under the police's nose was insane. Dr. Nee had called the cards, and they were playing out just as he had said they would.

When Casey made no move to get out, Destin asked, "What is the plan?"

"You go in. You and Greg make the transfer, and I'll stay with the car."

"Are you mad?" Destin demanded. "I'm not going in without you."

"Why?" Casey glared at him. "Is there something in there you have set up for me?"

"Yes, a transfer of a million plus dollars. That is what we are here for. That is why I broke my wrist getting your supplies and stole this car for you in the middle of the night."

Casey shifted so his back was against the passenger door behind him. His gun was trained on Destin once more. "I say you go in."

"I'm getting used to this now," Destin answered sarcastically. "Shoot me, Casey. Then you can deal with my bloody body like I did for you. Or would you just dump me out here?" Destin's gaze did not waver. "Where does your loyalty lay, Mr. Heedmen? You have let Greg twist you against me. Edgar and I could have left you inside to die. We could have made a break for it and let it all fall on you. But I didn't, did I? How do you know it's not Greg pulling a quick one? He has all the resources. He's the one who has been running around the town free as a bird. Have you checked up on who he has been talking to?"

They glared at each other for a long minute before Destin broke the silence. "Greg is inside. Are we going in?"

———

Zach reached over and took Brook's hand, "Lord, we pray you would protect the police force tonight. Keep them from harm. Cause the minds of Casey and his men to be muddled. Blind them to the police's activity. Give them confidence so that they will walk unknowing into the trap. Jam their weapons and muddle their thoughts so that they cannot hurt these brave men who are there to stop them. You love justice, and we ask that you would allow justice to prevail. And Lord, would you use this to bring my dad to you? He knows the truth. Set him free. Amen."

"Amen," Brook met his eyes and smiled. "You prayed for

your dad, Zach. It wasn't just words, you really meant it."

Knowing what she was thinking, Zach smiled back, "I've had a lot of time to think, Brook. It hit me that Dad could have died out there tonight." Zach looked away, "He still could. I say I believe in God's forgiveness, but I don't live like it is strong enough to reach my dad. I know it will take time, but I've chosen to forgive him."

She squeezed his hand. "Well done, Zach."

———

Casey followed Destin into the building, his gun drawn. Greg had disarmed the doors. They moved confidently, knowing their presence would not be recorded as they made their way down the hall to the first office as planned.

Destin glanced around before tapping twice on the office door.

Greg opened it, looking relieved. "What took you so long," he hissed angrily.

"Skip it," Casey snapped.

Greg glanced between them and spotted the gun in Casey's hand. "Everything is set up for you."

"Destin will run it," Casey instructed, his face hard.

"Good time to learn the ropes, eh, Greg." Destin stepped up to the laptop on the desk. The log in screen popped up, and Destin looked back at Casey. "Mind logging me in?"

Casey stood considering.

"What's with you two?" Greg demanded, keeping his voice low. "You have a fight in the car? We are on a tight time schedule here if we want to get this money moved."

"What's your hurry, Greg?" Destin leaned against the desk and crossed his arms. "Are you expecting someone?"

"No." Greg's eyes grew fearful. "Casey you know I'm not. I don't know what he told you, but it's not true."

"You seem a little rattled," Destin pointed out.

"I've been waiting here for thirty minutes," he glanced at the clock and muttered, "Twenty, but it feels longer when you are in here wondering if you were left holding the bag. Come on, Casey, you know I'm not like that."

Casey's answer was slow and calculated. "You sure were quick to throw Destin under the bus. Now that the tables have turned, you do seem a little jumpy."

"The camera recording gives us 45 minutes, and we are 21 minutes in." Greg pointed out. "I can't restart it with us inside. People will notice the clocks are behind. We have to do this now or pull out."

"Fair point," Destin agreed. "What's it to be Casey? You want the money tonight or do you want to let Calgen's people keep it for a few more days?"

Casey moved forward with calculated movements. There was no longer trust between them, and the tension could be felt. All three knew that if something happened it would be every man for himself.

CHAPTER 32

"What do you think they are doing out there? It has been hours!"

The thin door at the end of the room opened, and Reese squeezed himself through back into the main room. "Could you have made that bathroom just a little smaller inside? I could almost still breathe when I shut the door."

The others grinned. They knew the reason they were together, and the common ground gave them a sense of unity. Sedge and Valarie were playing a revised version of checkers using the bottle tops and the bumps of plastic Brent had cut from the bottom of the bottles with his pocket knife. They had already exhausted tic-tac-toe.

"So, Brent, what do you do for a living?" Reese asked settling himself on the bench.

Valarie, who was facing that side of the room, glanced up with interest.

"I work for Dr. Nee. He is a brilliant professor with doctorates in several seemingly unrelated areas of study, psychology, electronics, and something dealing with brain development." Brent looked up at the cement ceiling as if he would find the words there. "Well, whatever that one is. There might be another. It will suffice to say that he is an incredible man."

"And what does your role in his company look like?" Reese rephrased the question.

"I mostly work on electronics. You could say it is my

passion." Brent was purposefully not meeting Valarie's curious gaze. "I love to push the edges of what people can do with electronics."

"Your turn," Sedge reminded her.

Valarie turned her eyes back to the game and moved a piece.

"Things like making cars that you can drive from a phone?" Reese would have liked to get a better look at the car.

"Yes, things like that. Things that might not ever get into the hands of the public but that can slip in and change a few lives."

"Sorry about your car," Sedge said over his shoulder. It had become an inside joke of sorts.

Brent moved over to where he could give Sedge a good brotherly shove. "Cut that out."

Sedge hopped Valarie's last piece and they moved to join the others. "If you ever make one of these safe rooms again, make it big. With a ping pong table,"

"And beds," Valarie added. She stretched out on the open end of the bench Reese occupied and put her heels up on the wall.

"And a full sized bathroom," Reese requested.

"I will make a note of your suggestions." Brent flourished his finger in the air as if writing something down.

Valarie laughed.

Brent looked at his phone. "The first layer of the swat team just entered the building." His eyes met Valarie's, and they both wished they could be there to help the police.

"I need to go to them," Brent rose and went to the trap door. All of the mirth was instantly gone from the little group.

Grabbing the box, he opened it and disabled the switch. "You keep it red," he instructed.

Valarie nodded seriously.

"Brent, be reasonable," Reese cautioned. "The federal

building is at least ten minutes from here."

"I can't believe I sat down here and let them move in without backup." Brent muttered, mentally kicking himself for not being more aware. He had let his guard down. More people would suffer because of his failure.

"You are too late to disable their gadgets."

Brent froze.

"I'm sorry to spill your secret like this," Reese went on. "But you have done your part. You need to let Dr. Nee and the police do the rest."

Sedge looked at the others, realizing he was the only one who had not known about Brent's power. "You were the one who disabled the robbery transfer before." He spoke softly as if in a dream. "You did it, but Casey saw me."

"I'm sorry, Sedge." Brent turned to face them. "There was nothing I could do about it. I didn't know you would come. You can't tell anyone. Or even let on that you know."

"Why?" Sedge asked skeptically. "You enjoy your freedom that much?"

"I have stopped a lot of crimes, and can go on stopping them as long as I can stay under cover." Brent looked them each in the eye as he spoke. "I'm one of the loose ends that would be tied up if any of them knew who had crossed them. I'm asking you to protect me." Their once jovial guide stood vulnerable before them. Suddenly, he was the one in danger, and the three he had saved now held his life in their hands.

———

Chief McKenzie's face was lit by the dim screen of the computer. Forrest Wilton, the heavy set president of the bank, stood to his right. Between them, and closer to the computer, was the head bank teller, Dean Jackson. He was a short man with prominent ears and greying hair.

"Any activity?" McKenzie asked, giving his eyes a break

from the screen.

"Nothing yet, Sir," Dean replied crisply.

Chief McKenzie tapped his fist against his open hand impatiently. "They are almost 30 minutes behind schedule. We need that flag to move. And you are sure there is no way to freeze your screen while they do the transfer?"

"Our bank prides itself on its excellent cyber security, Mr. McKenzie." Wilton looked at the police chief with a hint of scorn.

McKenzie pointed at the corner of the screen. "I was only wondering because your computer is two minutes behind."

Dean's fingers flew over the keys, but the screen did not change.

McKenzie grabbed his radio. "They are in. Move in now. I repeat, unit one move in immediately."

———

"The connection was interrupted." Destin met Casey's eyes. Both men could almost taste the fear of the other. It was as if they were reliving the past.

This was exactly how it had happened six years before. An instant later they heard the heavy outside door swing open.

"Get out of here!" Destin hissed, scrambling to shove the equipment into the briefcase.

"One of you crossed me." Casey's gun swung from one to the other.

Greg spun to face him. "No, Casey, no," he pleaded backing toward the door.

"Not now, Casey, we have to get out of here." Destin attempted to sling the strap over his shoulder, intending to grab the laptop with his right hand. His wrist gave out and the bag fell with a thud to the floor. His face contorted with pain, Destin shoved the laptop into Casey's free hand, "Get out and get rid of this!" he urged frantically.

"Someone crossed me," Casey repeated, his eyes wild.

Destin grabbed the bag with his good hand as the office door burst open. A smoke grenade landed in the middle of the room sending out a billowing cloud of choking smoke.

"This is the police. Come out with your hands up." Came the strong command from the hall.

The room instantly erupted with gunfire. Destin cried out and slumped forward into the desk, knocking a cup of pens to the floor with him as he slid lifelessly to the carpet.

Greg cried out in pain and fell halfway through the doorway. "Don't leave me, Casey!" he shouted desperately.

Without a word, Casey shot Greg where he lay. He tossed the computer through the smoke toward where he had seen Destin fall. They would take the rap on this one. Stepping over Greg's body, Casey sprinted down the hall away from the main lobby. The smoke from the grenade gave him enough cover in the confusion to get away. There was an emergency exit at the back of the building. He saw the glowing exit sign ahead. Pushing it open he looked out into the blackness. For one second, everything was still. The next instant, the silence was pierced by the deafening alarm.

Casey ducked and ran for the decorative row of bushes. As he neared them, the shadows shifted and turned into shapes of men in black uniforms.

Casey's gunshot was barely noticeable above the sound of the blaring alarm. The swat team swarmed Casey, tackling him to the ground and wrenching the gun from his hand. Casey was handcuffed and jerked roughly to his feet. They searched him, removing a spare ammo clip and a knife from his pockets.

As they transported him to the front of the building, the chatter in their earpieces informed the unit that the three they were after had been accounted for and secured. The all clear was sent over the radio.

Chief McKenzie was waiting out front. "I have waited a long time for this, Heedmen."

Casey glared at him defiantly. "You have no evidence. I will be a free man tomorrow."

"We were very careful about that this time," McKenzie informed him coolly. "We will see what the judge has to say about it." He stepped aside. "Take him away."

CHAPTER 33

The trap door lifted from the top and the four inside the safe room blinked up in surprise.

"Mom!" Valarie squirmed past the others. Scrambling up the stairs, she passed the officers, threw her arms around Brook, and clung to her.

Brook held her daughter tightly.

Valarie reached out, and Zach squeezed her hand. "Thank the Lord you are okay."

The others emerged, looking out of place in the crowd of police. Zach went forward and hugged Reese. "I'm glad you are okay, Dad."

Reese hugged him back. They stepped apart, and Reese pulled his son aside. "Zach, down there I saw first-hand how hard it was for Valarie to wait, not knowing if she would see you again. I understood for the first time how you must have felt growing up."

Zach blinked hard, his eyes suddenly moist. "It's fine, Dad."

"No, Zach. It is not fine." Reese looked Zach in the eye. "You spent years waiting for me. Never knowing if I would come home again. And when I did come home, I never had time for you. I missed you growing up. Once you were a teen, you didn't want anything to do with me. Understandable but awkward, as if I were sharing my house with a stranger."

Zach wiped his eyes.

"I guess what I'm saying is that I'm sorry I wasn't there

for you." Reese cleared his throat gruffly. "Would you forgive me?"

Zach nodded, wiping his eyes again.

Reese pulled his son into another hug.

"We still have time, Dad. Let's not be strangers anymore."

"I would like that."

"Reese, I'm sorry to interrupt. We want to get you all down to headquarters to take your statements. While things are still fresh."

"But they are exhausted," Brook protested. "Can't it wait until tomorrow?"

Valarie looked up at her, smiling through her tears, "Mom, it is tomorrow."

———

Brent sat chewing the inside of his lip. He had given his statement, keeping it brief and to the point. Having signed the papers to decline a medical examination, he now sat in the private waiting area for the others to finish. He could have left, and almost had several times. But he had to know if they had told his secret. He needed to know if he would leave as a hunted man.

"Brent, right?"

Startled, Brent looked up to see Valarie's dad standing a polite distance away. Instantly, Brent wondered if the distance was out of respect or fear of his once secret abilities.

"You looked kind of lost in thought, so I didn't want to startle you."

"Yes, I'm Brent." He stood and offered his hand.

They shook hands.

"You've changed since we last met," Zach observed, causing Brent to shift uncomfortably. He gestured to where Brent had been sitting. "Mind if I join you?"

"Sure." Brent sat again, unsure of what else to say.

"Thank you for what you did for Valarie and my dad." Zach's eyes grew moist. Looking away he blinked to clear them. "Sorry."

"It's okay. I guess it was a long day for us all." Brent wished he had followed his instinct and left.

"You risked your life for two people who mean the world to me," Zach tried again. "I wanted you to know how grateful we are to you."

Brent nodded, "I'm glad it all worked out."

"They told me the story. About you saving Sedgewick and all. That was a noble thing to do."

"Did they tell you why?" Brent decided it was better to know than to wonder.

"Yes."

Brent's heart sank.

"Because you work for Dr. Nee. What an incredible job to have! I admit, I underestimated him and the work he does. I see now that he could not disclose all that his research accomplishes. This world needs more people like you who use their talents to help others."

Brent had hoped for more information, but now found himself unsure of what the information meant.

"Brent?" Dr. Nee strode towards him. Even though they had been up all night, Dr. Nee still looked crisp and sharp in his tailored black suit. "They said you are free to go. I will give you a ride if you like."

"Yes, please." Brent rose and shook Zach's hand awkwardly. "Tell Valarie and the others goodbye for me if you see them. I mean…"

Zach laughed and the awkwardness fell away. "I know what you mean. Thanks again, Brent."

———

Once they were in the car, Brent leaned his head back

against the headrest with a sigh.

"You did well, Brent," Dr. Nee said, pulling away from the police headquarters. "Three lives were saved because of your bravery and skill."

Brent smiled wearily. "Do you know if they told about my..."

Dr. Nee glanced over at Brent when he did not finish. "They did not. Your secret is safe."

Brent let his breath out. "With that many people knowing, it will get out eventually. At least I will have a few more productive years left."

Dr. Nee laughed. "I pray you have many productive years yet. There are many people who need our help. The team is packing up for the next assignment now."

"I was hoping to sleep for at least a week," Brent complained good-naturedly.

They drove in silence for a few minutes.

"No one would tell me what happened in the federal building," Brent observed. "Did Destin make it?"

Though Dr. Nee did not take his eyes from the road, Brent saw a smile change the shape of his face.

"He's on to the next assignment, then?"

"Casey thinks he shot Destin." Dr. Nee's eyes shone with victory. "As far as he knows, Destin is dead."

Shifting to see the professor better, Brent pressed for more information.

"Years ago, the barrel of the gun Casey carries was altered ever so slightly so that the bullet cannot travel in a straight line."

Brent laughed. "That's why he missed Detective Calgen?"

Dr. Nee nodded.

"And he used the same gun for the second attempt?"

"He used one Destin gave him years ago. It too had been altered slightly to better fit our purpose. The news will report that Casey killed both of his men. We will not tell them any different."

"You think of everything!"

"One must think of everything when anything not thought of could mean death."

"Is that a Chinese proverb?" Brent asked with a laugh.

Dr. Nee glanced over at him. "If I am Chinese and I say it, it becomes a proverb."

Laughing felt good. Brent had not realized the weight of pressure he had been carrying until it was lifted. "How did it happen? How did Destin escape?"

The light turned green, and Dr. Nee crossed the intersection before answering. "After you secured the three and Casey realized he could not get to them, he 'cracked up'. In psychology we have another word for it, but Destin says that is the proper term for losing one's nerve or ability to think clearly under pressure. Have you heard of it before?"

"Yeah, it is pretty common in old detective movies," Brent agreed.

"I do not watch them," Dr. Nee informed him. "However, it is what Destin says happened to Casey. He suspected Destin was an informer. Once he could not take the revenge he had planned, his mind become obsessed with the fear that one of his men would cross him. It is how he came to attempt a second robbery using the same method as before. Only this time, the police were ready to stop him."

"But what about the connection failing? How did that happen?"

"It was a very strange thing," Dr. Nee told him, pulling into the parking lot of the warehouse they had rented for the past 8 months. "It seemed as if you yourself were there." Dr. Nee pushed open his door and got out. "It could have been a problem with internet."

Brent's eyes widened, and he jumped out of the car.

Running to catch up with Dr. Nee, he put his hand on the small man's arm to stop him.

"It was you, wasn't it?" he asked, searching the professor's eyes for any clues. "You can control electricity too. That is how you were able to coach me so well in honing my gifts."

Dr. Nee smiled and patted his hand. "You are tired, Brent. Get some rest while the others pack. I must attend to my office."

Brent stood looking after the professor in amazement.

CHAPTER 34

"Jessie!" Squealing with delight, Valarie hugged her friend tightly. A week had passed since their ordeal, yet it already felt like it had all been part of a strange dream.

"I was really scared I wouldn't see you again." Jessie hugged her again.

"Why do girls have to squeal?" eight-year-old Micah asked as he entered the room.

"Because we are so happy that the happiness is compressed into sound and shoots out through our throats," Jessie told him with a suppressed grin.

"It does not." Micah retrieved his book and left the room.

Valarie pulled Jessie to the couch, and they sat side by side. "Micah checks every so often to see if I'm still here," Valarie whispered with a glance toward the hall. "He leaves that book around so I won't catch on."

Jessie giggled. "That's so sweet." She pulled up one leg and turned to see her friend better. "Tell me all about everything! It is all over the news. People can't talk about anything else. The biggest crime ring ever has been broken up. The fringe members are being picked up all over in so many different states. And you were part of it!"

"Apparently, Brent designed something that can detect that kind of hacking and break the signal. Or maybe his machine just detects it and gives a warning?" Valarie laughed. "I have no facts, but there's the story."

Jessie laughed too. "They say the judge gave Casey Heedmen the biggest punishment possible. They had enough evidence on him to put him away for ages. He shot both his men and tried to get out, but the swat team got him." Jessie gripped Valarie's arm. "Tell me the scariest part."

Valarie grinned. Hugging the couch cushion, she launched into a detailed description of the wild car ride.

Jessie was listening, wide eyed, when Zach pushed open the front door and entered with Trent, Valarie's gangly teenage brother.

"Hi Valarie. Hi Jessie." Trent greeted them as he passed them on the way to his room.

"Hi Trent!" they answered cheerfully.

"What is all this?" Zach looked into the living room with a smile. "You girls catching up after a long week of absence?"

"I missed Jessie so much Dad!" Valarie answered exuberantly. Noticing her Dad's sunburned face, she asked, "How was fishing?" Fishing was a new hobby her dad was trying to start with her Grandpa.

Reese entered in time to catch her question. "I think there's not a fish bigger than a minnow in that whole pond," he complained. "But your dad did catch one of them."

"It wasn't a minnow. It was a certified trout," Zach corrected from the kitchen. He came back drying his hands on the dish towel.

Holding up his fingers only an inch apart, Reese agreed with a smirk.

"How about those news headlines? Did you girls see them?" Zach moved his hand in an arch as if reading a headline. "Retired Detective Gets His Man After Six Years."

Reese drew his shoulders back slightly, proud that the papers had given him some credit for the conviction of Casey Heedmen. Not one for the limelight, he quickly shifted the subject. "Tomorrow the paper will read, 'Retired Detective's

Son Catches Minnow.'"

The girls laughed heartily at his joke.

Zach grinned at his dad, glad for the chance to have his father as a friend.

"Let's go clean up the tackle before all that slime gets dried on," Reese suggested.

"Trent?" Zach called as they headed out the front door together.

Trent, looking tired and hot, passed the girls again on his way to help put things away.

"Did you have fun?" Valarie asked.

He paused and looked thoughtful. "It was fun to see Dad and Grandpa joking about stuff." He started to leave but paused in the doorway. "I'm really glad you are safe, Valarie." He hurried out before she could respond.

"Aw! That was really sweet." Jessie meant it.

"Trent is growing up into a fine young man," Valarie said, masking the emotions the simple statement had invoked.

"What about you? Any new growing up plans involving Brent?"

Valarie made a face. "Don't be awkward, Jessie. Brent is like 25 years old."

Jessie shoved her with a laugh. "I wasn't asking if you were going to marry him, Valarie. He's nice, but he's ancient!" She laughed again at Valarie's obvious relief. "Are you going to go work for Dr. Nee?"

Valarie's eyes lit up with anticipation. "You can't tell a soul."

"Not this again!" Jessie groaned. "You know I don't tell unless you are in danger."

"I still have to say it," Valarie reminded her friend. Lowering her voice, she said, "I don't know yet. I have to finish school for now. But I will be old enough to officially sign on when I'm 18."

"And before that?" Jessie could see the excitement in

Valarie's dark brown eyes.

"Who knows, Jessie. Dr. Nee said he would contact me if something came up."

———

Brent adjusted his sunglasses. It was the end of the day, and the sun rays seemed to shine right into the windshield of his black car. For a moment, he turned his attention from the clinic door to the long, deep scratches on the inside panel of his door. Running his finger along the deepest mark, Brent shook his head. When he had time, he would have to get the damage repaired.

His eyes returned to the clinic door in time to see Destin emerge with an olive green cast on his wrist and lower arm. Destin had been right about the break. They were a day's travel from the city at a little country clinic where their presence would not be as noticeable. Brent was hoping their record keeper was as dedicated as their painter. The building's once blue paint was peeling terribly leaving stretches of off-white where it was missing all together.

Destin slid in and looked over at Brent. "I was not expecting you in this," Destin confessed. "What about the whole secrecy move thing?"

"This is secret." Brent answered, putting the car in gear. "What did they say about your wrist?"

"It is broken. I suspected it was. So now I have a fancy, expensive cast." Destin buckled his seatbelt as they pulled out into traffic. "I guess I was not as invincible as I thought."

"Not invincible, but a highly skilled man," Brent observed. "But why not stop Casey when he was shot all those years ago?"

Brent glanced over to see how he took the question.

Destin did not have to consider the question. "That I can answer in one word, Edgar. Edgar held the gang together.

When Casey was shot, Edgar and I got to him at the same time. Casey is dangerous because he is patient and never lets go of a grudge. His weakness is that he tends to react impulsively when he doesn't get what he wants. Edgar on the other hand is smart, good with a gun, and loyal to the core. The only thing I could do was go along with Edgar's plan to save Casey and hope for another chance. I was fairly new in the gang at that time and knew blowing my cover would send them all out of reach."

"And you to your grave?" Brent grinned, keeping his attention on the road.

"That too," Destin agreed seriously. "It was a tight line to walk."

"So you got Edgar arrested up front to get him out of the way this time," observed Brent coolly.

"I believe the credit for that goes to Dr. Nee." Destin's eyes scanned the countryside they were driving through.

Brent glanced over when Destin fell silent, "You alright?"

"Yeah," Destin answered distractedly. "Now that I'm dead, I'm going to have to figure out what to do with the rest of my life."

Grinning, Brent adjusted his sunglasses. "I know a great boss if you are interested in a fast-paced line of work."

STRENGTH OF SILENCE

Eddie stayed where he was, listening. In the distance, a motor started up. He waited until it had faded before he stood. Dizziness washed over him, and he steadied himself against the counter. Still moving unsteadily, Eddie removed the floorboards and laid them aside. He heard something out front and froze. If the police caught him here, there would be no end of trouble. Moving toward the back door Eddie pushed it open. Outside, trash cans and a variety of other things littered the yard. A car motor rumbled toward him, and Eddie ran.

JASON ROPER

Infused with invincibility and trained for greatness, Jason Roper is set to fulfill his father's dreams. But when Roper deviates from the instructions he is given, he stumbles upon an expansive criminal network. Determined to use his power to help those in need, Jason Roper discovers that there are times when invincibility alone is not enough.

Is Jason Roper destined for greatness as he has been told, or is his life just a front for a larger, more sinister plan?

Roper Returns

Jason Roper's second mission is clear-cut. He moves in with confidence, feeling invincible and unstoppable. But things are not what they appear on the surface. Even his invincibility has limits Roper did not know.

With no one to turn to, Roper finds himself sinking into a darkness he does not have the power to evade.

The Man Behind The Melody

The unexpected death of his twin sister threw Mark into a whirlwind of change. Disowned by his stepfather, Mark set out with only one goal in mind, to get as far away from the hateful man as possible. He clung desperately to the last link with his sister, her saxophone. Wandering the streets, Mark's path crossed with a stranger who could see potential no one else could see. Mark, an unwanted orphan, was offered the chance to become more than he had ever dreamed. But could the stranger be trusted?

CARBON
An Unforgettable Adventure

Carbon slipped out of bed and turned on the light. Taking a sheet of thick drawing paper from her desk she drew the face of the man the article simply called Roper. Pulling the picture she had drawn earlier from her file box, she laid them side by side on the desk. It was little or nothing to go on. The prisoner could have been a thousand different people. She had no face to compare. Suddenly the image of the stranger in the alley came to mind and Carbon frowned thoughtfully. He was the only one who would know.

ROPER

Protecting his family was Jason Roper's top priority. When his identity is exposed by a bullet that should have taken his life, Roper scrambles to try to protect the ones he loves most. Only this time, it is him they are after.